KISSED BY

KISSED BY ALEXANDRA CHASIN

FC2

TUSCALOOSA

The University of Alabama Press
Tuscaloosa, Alabama 35487-0380

Published by FC2, an imprint of the University of Alabama Press, with support provided by Florida State University and the Publications Unit of the Department of English at Illinois State University

Address all editorial inquiries to: Fiction Collective Two, Florida State University, c/o English Department, Tallahassee, FL 32306-1580

⊗

The paper on which this book is printed meets the minimum require-ments of American National Standard for Information Sciences—Per-manence of Paper for Printed Library Materials, ANSI Z39.48–1984

Library of Congress Cataloging-in-Publication Data
Chasin, Alexandra.
   Kissed by / by Alexandra Chasin. — 1st ed.
      p. cm.
   A collection of innovative fictions.
   ISBN-13 978-1-57366-138-6 (pbk. : alk. paper)
   ISBN-10: 1-57366-138-4
   I. Title.
   PS3603.H3797K57 2007
   813'.6—dc22
                                        2007016013
Cover Design: Lou Robinson
Book Design: Tara Reeser
Typeface: Baskerville
Produced and printed in the United States of America

Acknowledgements of previous publication:

"Two Alphabets," *Denver Quarterly* 41.4, 2007

"Potatoes, You Ask," *elimae*, December 2006

"all kinds of people on the Q train," *sleepingfish* 0.875, 2006

"Kant Get Enough," *Exquisite Corpse*, Winter 2004

"The Mystery of Which Mystery," *Phoebe* 32:2, Autumn 2003

"Why I'm Jealous," *West Branch* 52, Spring 2003

"ELENA=AGAIN," *DIAGRAM* 2.6, Winter 2003

"Toward A Grammar of Guilt," *The Capilano Review* 2:36, Winter 2002

dedicated to

judith butler, mary jean corbett
& ira livingston

who keep me
(strange)

Contents

Kissed By

I began as we all do, by wanting something, but I hardly knew what. I began by wanting somebody, nobody, everybody to know that I wanted something, but I hardly knew which. I considered all the others that had ever been drawn or withdrawn from life, like me. There was, among them, a little bird. It flew around the inside of an airport. Elsewhere, even farther from the frame, there was an alcoholic white woman waiting for a wedding ceremony to end. There was one first kiss, or should I say two? How many kisses are there in a first kiss?

I began as all we sketches do by wanting something or someone made up. But there's no such thing.

I was begun by an artist so abstract or minimalist or simply wrong-minded that I HAVE NO FACE.

In the beginning, I wanted to be by a painter who has three easels going at once, each on another wall, like Roz in her studio in the Bowery with one small pastel and two big paintings in various stages of existence so that when she comes to the temporary end of one of the oils, when in her mind its maroon of the moment has been exhausted, she can turn to the right, pick up the pastel fresh and apply the curves she just began to know it needed when she was up to her wrists in red a minute before and a quarter-turn ago.

Like the witch in *The Patchwork Girl of Oz*, who stirs all four pots at once, one with each limb. But constantly. Can you see her now, wooden spoons with long handles, handles tied with rags to her forearms and shins, two rags around each stirring part, wound double tight? Head drooping with fatigue, straw hanging wearily from her pointy noggin, oh so tired, still she stirs.

Like Moira Shearer trapped in *The Red Shoes* whose bad magic consists in compelling their wearer to dance. But forever. Ceaseless pirouette, vertiginous arabesque. A night, a spinning fortnight, an unearthly long time, until she dances down to the station, out on the tracks, and under a train.

So I turned to my scarlet artist and begged and begged for words and birds and weddings. Unbelievably, she agreed to a few strokes. But she is a brute and leaves me faceless. She gives me leave to stray because I'm not too hard to find. She lets me drive a car, but when I pull up at a stoplight, the drivers in the cars stopped around me look away or look again with horror. If she's not careful, I will cause an accident and if she *is* careful, I will cause an accident. And when and when and how and how will I ever get my kiss?

I might take an epic journey which I might begin by stumbling through Gate 22 and onto a flight to a faraway place to watch my sister follow a pink flower child down the aisle and into the curving arms of a fearsome man. I might see my mother lurch to the dance floor to do the Funky Tradition, hours after *I do* has been said and seconds after my sister has taken her last happy twirl. I might spirit away the flower child and we might head eternally for the tangerine on the horizon as it eludes us west and west again.

But that would be an easy out—too watercolor, too insipid for my painter. She would have me faceless fodder. She is terrible.

I begged again for the concrete. She taunted me: Wood a paintbrush do, souring in turpentine? Wood a very long-handled spoon?

Wood this unfinished block at the tip of toe shoes do? Wood you rather your sister walked some pirate plank and fell into the Dead Red Sea? She laughs while I rack up splinters in my unfisted hands.

So I dropped by Roz's studio, hunched like the headless horseman to protect the fine-feathered figure in the lobby. I rang once, I rang twice. Either Roz had the music up too high or she had herself up too high. Or maybe she was home in bed kissing as long as she knew it would take the vermilion of the day before to dry. What is the color of one Roz kissing.

What are two weeks spent spilling out of ruby slippers as against a lifetime of sneaking around without a face? Why can't I hot-air-balloon it out of town instead of facing: the earnest east, its early-to-bed-early-to-rise philosophy of life; the music without mercy; the plain fact that a griddle can spit better than I can? Why does she paint me into the corner of complaint, smiling all the while? She, she has and does and says it all.

About all I can really say for myself? Caucasian. Beyond that, it's a blur. All I can really say is, it hurts, but not in my eyes or nose or mouth. All I can say is, I could go on forever. All I can finally say is, I would throw myself under the crimson canvas for just two plummy kisses.

The Mystery of Which Mystery

Some elements I want in my story:

I would like seduction without commitment; dubious intentions; groundless, but nonetheless debilitating, doubt. Of course, they've been done before.

I'm considering children separated from their parents, having been abandoned, abducted, left temporarily in someone's care, or having wandered away—in any event, the parent, the pivot point of consciousness, somehow suddenly gone.

I'm thinking of Leo, thinking of Lise. Maybe you'd like to know what I think they think.

I'll need the laundromat, the department store, the riverbank, the amusement park, the bus terminal, and maybe the train station, places where grownups can vanish. Watch with me while Leo wonders, as he has done so many times before, why his mother picked the laundromat, of all places, to take off from. The one of the above that most seems to promise a return. When the coins are spent and the cycle done. A blue whale is beached on the wall. Why did she work it out so that Leo would spend forty-five minutes without any doubt that she would come back to put the clothes in the dryer, without the slightest hint that she might not be back to scoop them, warm and dry, another hour after that, into the big canvas sack, to take them, and him, home together? In retrospect, Leo thanks her for those forty-five minutes. At the

15

time, Leo put the wet wash in the dryer by himself, and fed it money, still without wondering. The blue whale blew bubbles. In retrospect, Leo can see that it was strange that she had left him three quarters, as though she meant to leave him with something, at least—enough money to take the bus across town, or enough clean clothes for a week, but not both. She didn't usually leave him with change, so Leo might have known, if he'd been paying more attention, that something was off. But because he did not know, he dried the clothes, and when he had waited long enough and the wash had set into wrinkles in the sack, Leo had no choice but to walk.

I want lovers, true lovers and false lovers and true/false lovers and too true/too false lovers, with other lovers of their own. Like when the only color in the scene on a midwinter midafternoon, which is otherwise white with snow, and dark with mud and clouds and lack of sun, when the only color at all is the naked brown of the trunk of a tree in the park. The wet-from-snow-melt rich dark earth brown, wearing the hard skin of a tree. Love that tells a story, saying that nut-bark brown is the very color of her hair. Love that true and false.

Don't you want lovers too?

I'd really get off on a missing hand, but I saw that in a play by Suzan-Lori Parks, so I can't use that.

I need mystery, I think. Not where Leo walked to, with his clothes in a sack, not that mystery. Not why his mother disappeared, not that mystery. Not love, that mystery.

Leo is older now, and now he has a girlfriend, Lise, whom he loves with all of his tattered heart. He passes by the old laundromat where the blue whale's bubbles have faded to tears. Lise's hair, shades of walnut, hangs down past her shoulders. Now Leo works as a reservations agent for Freewheeling Travel Agency. Lise is a dancer, so in between rehearsals and performances, she teaches dance to girls and boys. She'd like to go places. Leo would like to take her there.

There has to be a river, an Ohio kind of river, down by the banks of which Willie stabs the girl who refuses to marry him, in the song. There has to be a river on which pucks slide in winter, in which mistakes sink in spring, across which animals and people swim and swim and come to rest. The requisite rubber tire will lie on the bottom and we'll just have to believe it's there because we'll never see it ourselves. It is, most assuredly, there. A river less polluted than it was thirty years ago, with a tire that first preceded, and then escaped, the clean-up. A good old river like the Old Man River kind of river, that just keeps rolling along. This river is green and blue and mudbottom brown but for one moment at sunrise when the river is yellow, and for one at sunset when it is red. There are trees by the river, which is very public, if never the same twice, and along which all the people in town sooner or later go walking. There is a handful of private spots: a grove of trees more dense than the others, the cave at the water's edge, the cement ledge shoring up the mudbank under the bridge. Lise and Leo have spent some time in these resort locales. We could meet at one, if you have the time, and peek in on them.

Not the source of the doubt, that's no mystery.

I'd like Leo to be okay, not to have been too badly hurt by what happened to him as a child, but it wouldn't be realistic. If he works three more months at the agency, though, he will be entitled to a ticket of some kind, free.

I've chosen a setting other than San Diego. San Diego is by the ocean, but it has no rivers, only creeks, and they're dry.

Setting the statue in motion.

Why don't you join me on this unseasonably warm February afternoon on a riverbank far from San Diego? Pigeons abound here, clocking from up in the leafless trees, leaving trident tracks amok in the mud. We could spy on Lise and Leo as they go walking in the park. Before he worked at Freewheeling, Leo played the town founder, his clothes spray-painted, and his face made-up in, the silver of statuary. He would stand still on a white plaster pedestal until someone, a spectator or a passerby, put a coin in the box on the ground. Then he would move just enough to smile or wink at that person and freeze again in a new official position. One day, Lise passed by. Since she first saw him there in his painted togs last May, Lise has wanted him wanted him wanted him. For Leo's part, he didn't even need to be wanted before he wanted wanted wanted her. He had already been struck by the approach of a girl who seemed to skate more than walk, whose hair flickered. In fact, she did not pass by him; she circled him, and coming to stand in front of him once more threw into his collection box every coin she had on her person—luckily, less than a dollar in change—one every ten seconds, to try to get him to dance, laughing as she did. They joked about it later. But at the time, Leo's marble skin wrinkled with fear. All he could think to do was jump down, take off his silver wreath, and crown her tree-bark head with it, which broke the remaining ice beautifully.

In a town whose tourism sends people away rather than brings them in, this line of work was not promising. Except that it brought Leo Lise.

Look, just now, Leo leans up against a tree, looking down on the river. Lise walks her right leg in toward his. Lise tells her sap it's not yet spring, but it doesn't believe her—and rises. Leo splays the fingers of Lise's right hand with his own. He offers her his neck, pulse first. Lise admires the grace of her left hand snaking up and over his shoulder. Lise and Leo could pique more than our curiosity, if you see what I mean.

Later, Lise goes to class. She takes a class and she teaches a class. Leo works at Freewheeling, putting together everybody else's travel packages. On the wall by his desk, a handprint in blue paint, Lise's. She gave it to him the day after a night that they woke up holding hands; both of them lay there, unspeaking and unmoving, each afraid to wake the other into an instinctual unlacing. Lise walks back from her classes; the river is for an instant red; night falls; she goes to meet Leo. He smiles when he sees her. He smiles when he enters her too, but right before he comes, his face looks like rage, which is the most exciting part to Lise. Right before Lise comes, she stops breathing; it's right before she doesn't come that her face looks like rage to Leo, which frightens him. Lise tells Leo that her dance company is set to start rehearsals for a new piece, to be premiered in eight weeks and in San Diego, worlds away.

The mystery of which mystery. That mystery.

There is a new guy in Lise's company. He's straight, judging by the existence of his ex-girlfriend, who hangs around rehearsals a lot, as though she doesn't have anything to do. She must be a student. Her ex-boyfriend, the new member of the troupe, has sandy hair and a background in improv. In his free time, he parachutes, as though he has less than nothing to lose, for which the director chastises him. No risks to life and limb is one of the rules of the

19

troupe. The new member laughs a lot. Lise behaves no differently than she ever did. But what does that mean?

In eight weeks, Freewheeling will be in peak season and Leo doesn't need to ask to know that he will not be given time off.

It's instant Shakespeare. Enter the sandy-haired guy—I'll call him Will. Think of the grove and the sap and the youth and the stage on which these players dance and play. Think of the tiptoe and prancing of fairies in the woods, beside which mortals, even dancing ones, look clumsy and wrong, like beached blue whales. Think of the silly games, funny to the fairies, that ruin people's lives.

Lise doesn't speak about Will when she and Leo decide that they don't have enough money to go in on a car together, even though a friend is offering an old one to them for cheap. But they can't afford the new tires it will need, nor the insurance. Lise and Will have a *pas de deux* that lasts for four minutes and twenty-eight seconds.

I wish I could introduce a device to divert Lise and Leo from their likely courses of action. But the only thing I can think of to save them now is a semaphore, and what does that mean? I've been told not to use words whose meaning might be unclear, but I can't reveal the source of the prohibition.

Lise doesn't mention Will when she and Leo wobble their way out of bumper cars. That's what worries Leo. She doesn't mention Will when Leo goes with her to buy a new duffel bag for her upcoming tour. Lise calls back to Leo in bed, "Watch," as she shows him her half of the duet, her eyes on the bedroom mirror.

She moves like mercury, like she could slide at the speed of silver or split herself into a million little bubbles. How can he hope to hold her? She has already streaked her beautiful brown hair with dubious blonde highlights.

But how too can he stand to watch her climb into the train along with her duffel bag, and Will, and his duffel bag, and the other dancers bound for San Diego?

A week before she is due to leave, Leo begins to panic. How can Will be disappeared, or turned into a toad? How can Leo live in this landlocked town without Lise, even for a few weeks? How can he stand on a platform, desperately trying to avoid the blatant symbolism of Will's ex-girlfriend standing there next to him? How can he stand to see Lise's joy as the train rolls friction-free to the west? It is too much, he cannot.

These are the mysteries Leo faces in April. They sink him even deeper into perplexity than he has been before. Any one of us can slide at any time, with or without the bells and whistles doppling down the track, with or without meaning to. By the same token, we run the risk of being left too abruptly—for example, the way I leave you here and now, wondering whether Leo uses his six remaining days to plot and execute the kind of crime that will keep Lise and Will apart forever, or turns his back on the platform to hurt Lise just a little as she waves out the window, goodbye, goes home to throw his old clothes in his own sort of a suitcase and carries it, in the yellow-rivered dawn of the following day, past the crying whale in the sleeping laundromat, to the bus station, to take his chances east.

Lynette, Your Uniqueness

I. WHERE THERE'S A WILL...

Reader, if you're looking for someone who missed you and still does, looking to have been found and lost and to be looked for again, read this page of *Missed Connections*. If you're hoping to be meant by a message or a sign, you might peruse *Crossed Signals*. If the precipitating contact was singular, and in the preterit, meaning just once, try *I Spy*. Maybe someone missed me, for example, an SWM, 35, licensed to practice architecture and other deceptions, or perhaps I crossed the mind of that certain someone who, the same him. If the contact was more than once, ongoing, incomplete, partial, imperfect, perfect, past perfect, final but unfinished, conditional, compromised by unpromising conditions, past conditional, depending on precisely what happened, try to forget or get over it.

Usually, they're kind of like this, the ads in all these columns:

THE 7-11 IN THE WEE OURS OF THE MORNING.
You: bleeding from a chest wound and then falling to
your knees. Me: stopped in for coffee, ended up w/
paper towels, absorbing your blackberry blood.
Was too wan to get your name.

So someone out there combed the convenience stores and then had this idea: Maybe fate is, just like history, a typesetter with an advertisement in hand. Why not believe, oh wan one? Why not shoot the purple-tipped arrow and hope it carries poison ink enough for two? Now, someone in here picks up the paper, smells the coffee, and tastes the wan one's misplaced hope, as the arrow falls out of the fold and clatters woodenly at her feet.

As always, the ghost of the me-and-you bird whistles through the frost. I hear nothing other than that, and see little else than the normal seasonal variations against the unfamiliar landscape: short snows that still melt quickly; the earth-brown ache still hanging on the trees, that will turn, by February, to gray; the stingy sun rounding the curve. I rotate and revolve, more furiously this year than last, attempting to plow the past year under. I ride the Ferris wheel down, waving a mitten at the pair of dragonflies in the silver bucket hanging opposite me on their way up.

Birdsong was once aloft. Now birdsong's trapped in here—it's cold out there.

II. THE ONES WHO GET AWAY

I respond to every Me, as though he or she were addressing little old me. I explain why it would not have worked out. Or I read as though I were You, the one the one The One Who Got Away, as they say. And/or I read him into Me, and I talk back, as I would have liked to do forever.

For example:

> 11/21, 5:35 P.M.: STANDING ON A CHAIR TO
> water a plant, you came within a hair's breadth of
> falling. I would have caught you. Gee, the odds?!
> 4801.

If this adster had caught me, odds are we would have had the kind of arrangement that that plant has with water; what the one would have given in nutrients, the other would have given back in green and semi-annual white, a give and take, but off-balance. It would never have been a cliché, not for one skinny minute. I could have promised you that but, chances are, it would have been the only promise kept between us, there in the hanging garden of our unlikely love.

Come April, we would have laughed like sorry hyenas at the pointlessness of the trees fruiting again this year.

Come night, we would have barked our little message of doom up at the moon just to hear the niblets shiver in their dewless skins. To hear the absence of the birdsong in the stubborn sapping tree.

III. YOU WHO

If you're looking for someone you missed, someone you miss, someone you found and lost and long for all over again, place your own ad. Mine would look like this:

Me: wild prairie grass August sun-lit out-buildings voles and a rainless July. You: a flint and a lot of hot air. Wanna dance?

In which I am Me and You remain abstract. In which there is no particular You. Or there is One, Who already Got Away.

I hear odd birds, a variety of species of wrong, unreal birds, and I misinterpret them to a tee. Every one a hummingbird, whirring in place, beating wings and tunes and singing me back my own messages with unerring echolalia.

When I cut myself, winter coming, on tips of things—arrows, feathers, and leaves that litter the living-room floor, sweep as I might—blood rushes, blue, to air. Dragonflies remember why.

IV. ...THERE'S (THE ONE WHO GOT) AWAY

If there had been justice, the me-and-you bird would right now have been pecking out your liver forever. You: rib-cage, naked, mythical, real, on the side of a stone cold mountain here in New England.

Where are you now? You, sung away.

Now birdsong is memory, which would have been news when the trees were still flush and I still lived down there and I still believed the things you said.

V. THE ONES WHO GOT A WAY

Sometimes, I try to establish certain conditions with the ad-placing strangers. For example, when I read:

> METRONOME 11/22. YOU: ADIDAS SHIRT AND
> shoes, brown hair, tats on left forearm (Japanimation).
> Me: All black, studded belt, dragonfly tat on chest,
> with the stick. Must see you again. 4803.

I explain what I want. I say: Can I see you without the stick? Or I imagine that I make a mistake for both of us:

> NORTH FORK/BIKE PATH WEDNESDAY.
> You: Stranded. I stopped, fixed your bike, we
> never said a word. Took-off before you could say
> thanks, but felt the depth of yr. "gratitude." Me:
> Pink shirt, "USMC" & pack. 4804.

I say: I see you now, black and brown features on a white face, glossy hair tilting the top of your head slightly to the left, cheekbones, lone dimple, a chin so strong it would make a Marine proud. Muscles would have been whispering out from under your shirt in abbreviated Latin: abs, pecs, delts, concave and flexing, purring *see me feel me* hairlessly, & pack or packing, either way. I would have turned, too late, to say: thank you, and: you have a look, a smile, a way, I like. You would have been two of the ones who got a way.

VI. THE ONE WHO GOT AWAY

You: the curly-haired aspiring architect who would have driven me home from an evening of music outdoors in a municipal park, me and you having earlier converged as strangers on the too-small blanket of a mutual friend, on a night that would have happened to be my birthday. Yours: the car in which I would have sat thinking: This is a righteous birthday gift, in between radio-musical kisses. Yours: the hard thigh, the dry palm, and the grackling eyes. Your vaguely continental accent peppering your tongue. Me: waiting for the phone to ring. Mine in the silence: the thought that if it didn't ring, that's how I would know it was you.

Now birdsong is newsprint; it papers my delicate cage.

VII. THE ONE WHO GOT AWAY

I would have poked fun at your accent in your car that night—that superbly musicked night—and I would have gone on to rib you about your fading accent long after you had been naturalized and your car had disintegrated into a pile of weightless flecks of rust, melting further away every time it rained.

Me: 30 by midnight. Me: remembering, which would have slipped into imagining, you for weeks. You: not calling until those weeks would have just about elapsed. You would have called a moment past the time when I would have said it was too late. But you: you could have wooed the me-and-you bird north in November. You would have.

VIII. WHITE FLIGHT

> PAT, INCREDIBLE POET! SAW YOU AT THE
> poetry slam at the Ennui 12/6. Haven't slept since.
> Can't forget your blue hair & sound of your voice.
> Let's go for a hot choc. with Bailey's, I bet that's
> your kind of drink. 4910.

If I were Pat, though I am not, my dye-job and I could not have been less impressed. If I were Pat, I'm guessing I would already

27

have had a lover, lolling at home, who cared for nothing so much as getting high; Bailey's would have made me gag; and anyway, dope would clearly have been my kind of drink. I would have taken the razor to the pure powdered cash in a trice, and would have sliced you just as soon, if you had lain on the mirror in lines.

When I moved beyond the birds and other UFOs, I came to where the cold is so extreme, it verges on comfortable. Down there, I contracted at the very thought of freezing; here, I walk late afternoons crunching the hard gray fog under a dark brown sky.

IX. YOOHOO

Me: reliable, columnar, Stonehenge. You: straw hat. No match. Irresistible, no?

X. DO YOU ME AND YOU?

Pathetic human birdsong printwise. *Homo sapiens sapiens* chatter chatter, nothing new under the oak:

Can I see you again? I must see you again. I can't sleep. Can I see you without your friends? I have to kiss you. I'm awake nights. You caught my eye. *Fly-by. Fly-by.* I can't eat. I haven't slept since. I just want to talk. Can we please try again? *Fly-by.* My breath catches just thinking. I must see you again. I can't forget you. I'd fly anywhere for you. *Fly-by. Fly-by.* I have to have one more dance with you. I must know. Can I take you to dinner? I'll never wash my hand. I can't sleep. I didn't get your number. Can I take you to a show? I should have gotten your number. Can we just take a walk in the daytime? Who are you?

Fly-by, the idiot bird with the hoping heart. Who spies and right away knows everything there is to know about the object of desire. For the mere cost of the words, sights are trained, bird beads are drawn, and purple arrows launched. And all without a little minute lost in idle perch.

While November ticks away on the wall, green divorcing leaves everywhere, I read in vain.

XI. THE ONES WHO GOD AWAY

> BLUE CHEVY REVELATION TO CONVENIENCE store in Burning Bush all the way from the Falls. 12 am 12/12. Isn't that a sign? White Blazer was intimidated, intrigued & flattered. Can we please try again? 5050.

It would have been uncharacteristic for this you to place such an ad, so trusting would this you usually have been in his or her God. For which reason, there would have been no point to anything between this you and the real me. Blue revelation pulled up and idling, pumping purple carbons right through the ozone layer. From the second I saw you across the parking lot, I would have seen the sacred heart flashing in your chest. I would not have been interested enough to find out what contradiction led you to publish your lack of faith. That would have been that right there.

I could shoot the messenger but I would still hear the rhythmic wingbeat all night all night all night long, sleep as I might. I could count each apparition of the dragonfly a miracle but I would be all wrong all wrong all wrong all wrong.

XII. ROLL CALL

If candlelight dinners make you sick and walks on the beach leave you cold, if films and flea markets are not worth getting out of bed for, and conversations are not worth staying in it for, give me a call. We'll have nothing to go on and on on. We can roller blade straight to hell and save a lot of time.

XIII. THE ONE WHO GOT AWAY

I would have explained my penchant for wood, stemming from its durability when built, which is shorter than stone but longer than a human life, thus all you'd ever need and not too much more. You said: Eventually the log cabin becomes the forest floor once more. I said: But before it does. If you had touched me then, and dangered me with fingers there—sublimed me with fire, as you would have done on our next date—but you would not, you would have nodded kindly and you would have shown me pictures of your buildings, which are never meant to be concrete, or built for real at all. It would have been hard to understand architectural designs that never go to engineers, but there they would have been: kohl-shadowed leanings twinkling with impermanence, defying form and function, the plane of the paper unequal to ground, elevations without sides, nothing anywhere so pedestrian as vents, godlings in the aerie attics, never in the details. Beautiful impossibilities. The raptor on your face would have made me miss the metaphor.

Now birdsong is my voice thrown up a tree for safekeeping. A tree's a place a bird calls home.

XIV. THE ONE WHO GOT AWAY

It is you who would have drawn me my tree house, finally, the tight place I always had in mind, where I am most I, and it would have slid to earth like sawdust, but it would have been the closest to real of any tree house I had ever had—hang though it did from imaginary rotating blades turning on vertical axes, and momentarily at that, unbranched all its short life long—and I would have toasted you for the gift even as I watched the realest ever treehouse cum hovercraft undissolve up off the ground, hook back

on to the shuttering blades, fake right, fake left, and snake away. I
would have heard a crazy bird in the empty distance...

TREEEEE!!!!!

XV. GRIEVING THE HOVERCRAFT

> 12/15 MONIQUE FROM WAITSVILLE? I SPY W/MY
> eye, someone who can fly, cheeks pink from windburn,
> you coming down off Mt. Hunger, wish I'd had
> the presence of mind to get your number! 5053.

Coming down off Mt. Hunger

Coming down off Mt. Empire State Building

Coming down off Mt. Nightmare

Coming down off Mt. Ferris Wheel

Coming down off Mt. Bad Experience

Coming down off Mt. Caffeine High

Coming down off Mt. Passionate Disingenuous Hatred of the
Last Lover I Had

...I would have been bound to be disoriented as I emerged
onto the plain.

A paper blanket for warmth, red ink, a new and steady job, a
new year on its way, according to the clock.

XVI. TALK IS CHEEP

The hopefuls who place these ads, do they not marvel at the
slimness of the chance that their star-crossed future-intended will
have even an inkling of a shimmer of an intuition that there's any
reason to read this column? And if the ones who were first sighted
and now might be getting away (unless they read the column) *did*
imagine that a purple-poison arrow was arcing toward them—if
they had also felt the whammy—why were they just sitting around

waiting for the other ones to place the ads, passively checking these pages once a week for signs that they were being looked for; why were they not following their bliss and searching out the ad-placers, haunting the original sites or placing ads themselves? It doesn't bode well.

XVII. DO YOU DO YOU DO YOU DO YOU WANNA DANCE?

Hopefuls hopping on fraying power lines:

We never said hello. I never thanked you. Who are you? I was too flustered, too flattered, too tongue-tied to ask you for your number. You never told me your real name. I want you bad. We never said thanks. I wonder. Can't we please try again. *Fly-by*. I'm so intrigued. I was short of breath. Can I see you without your clothes? I can't stop wondering. Where have you been all my life? We never said goodbye. *Fly-by*. *Fly-by*. I didn't have the presence of mind to get your number. I didn't catch your name. I have to know the name of the one who's got my breath. I don't have your number. I want to hold you. I can't stop wondering whether you're wondering too.

Only the fly-by bird says what it does and does what it says, its lyrics repetitive but honest. The fly-by bird, the one who hits and runs. Says what it does. Honest, but creepy and unrealistic.

XVIII. QUICKDRAW

Me: A sucker for singsong sweet talk, for desert dwellings carved out of or into dried mud in the hot sun, sympathetic with snails. You: slippery as graphite, too graphic to be true, shaded shavings underfoot, hands unsafe at any speed. Us: at home in the gloom.

XIX. THE ONE WHO GOT AWAY

I would have Lufthansa with you. Yellow Star Boat Lines, Royal Air Maroc, the ferry east from Ancona, buses over mountains shining with heat, and sixteen months later there would have been one last leg of a round-trip flight, Lufthansa with you once more. We would have sensed the globe beneath the earth, felt the arch in our backs when we slept, and woken again to hop from patch to patch on this great purple soccer ball. The places we could have gone. The going we could have complained about and enjoyed the hell out of: long lines; tomato and cheese sandwiches or fried dumplings; local currencies damp with sweat in our pockets; rain; fucking standing up, ankle deep in garbage; language barriers; and snow.

You with all those buildings in your head, the aspiring kind that slide into the sea when you draw them on paper, harder to fix on than cotton candy. Tall slender quasi-structures that wave in the wind like bamboo, until they slip rootlessly down...and the birds consequently flap up. What on earth would you have called the color of those houses, which is where aqua meets pink, opalescent, elusive as hell?

XX. BIRDS DO IT

I'd really like to think there could have been a fortuity of *Missed Connections*. One with me in it. Isn't it possible that an old lover missed me, that I crossed somebody's mind? Couldn't I have been the one, this week, who finally got away? For too many months, it's been the other way around, but couldn't luck turn right at any time? Couldn't good news be winging its way toward me right now? Maybe someone saw me from a distance last week; maybe I caught somebody's eye. I think I may have been the unwitting victim of

Crossed Signals. Couldn't I have been the unsuspecting object in a case of *I Spy?* Perhaps I'm forgetting an incidental encounter, an accidentally decent gesture on my own part; perhaps there was an unaccountable appeal in the way my umbrella inside-outed itself. I'd like to believe that there could have been an unusual occurrence, an anomaly, a serendipity of which I was unaware. Honk of trumpets. Destination: the beloved. Roses in my eye.

Why would we, the ones who might unfortunately be getting away, be reading this column unless we believed that good news might have recently originated with a mysterious stranger and be winging its way to the reader? Who among us would not bend down for the sand-encrusted bottle with a scrap of hope inside?

XXI. YOU DON'T FEEL YOU COULD LOVE ME, BUT I FEEL YOU COULD

> YOU KNOW WHO YOU ARE! YES YOU!! I HAVE had my eye on you for 27 years. I will love you forever. From the cradle to the gutter to the grave. Happy Birthday, Anniversary, Valentine, to my one & only. 12/16, 12/17 and every day. 5055.

Would that you had not long ago drunk away the money from the job you lost seven years before;

Would that you had washed your hair any time in the last two months;

Would that your one pair of pants had been stained anywhere but the crossroads of your crotch seams;

Would that you had, in your tattered valise, a now-am-found facial expression that you would have been able to try on from time to time to make sure it could still co-habit with your once-was-lost one;

Would that you had not attempted to ride the fly-by bird and thus grounded her the one and only time we would have met as adults in the gutter that leads to the grave, the self-same bird you would have shot at with the BB gun when we were kids;

I feel sure that I would have been able to love you deeply.

XXII. THE ONE WHO GOT AWAY

You would have taught me to drive a stick shift in an old Dodge Dart; you would have been the perfect teacher because you would have silently ulcerated rather than undermine my confidence as I drove out of the shopping center parking lot (where I would have stalled no less than eleven times before finally sliding into first gear and keeping the thing alive, if grumbling), down the avenue past the high school and the car wash and the concrete cathedral, around the back of the train station. You would have explained the social, economic, and of course, religious, implications of concrete. I would have stalled one last time at the merge into the rotary, the horizontal Ferris wheel. About the aesthetics of concrete, we would have argued late into the night, after I had turned the car off—the first time I would have done so on purpose all evening—after the engine dropped silently from hot to warm, but would we have fallen asleep before the car had cooled down to the temperature at which it might never have been driven at all? Or would we still have been considering the curvaceous quality of highway clover leaves and off-ramps, and the virtues of brutalism, and disagreeing about whether Western civilization declined in correlation with the introduction of cinder-block dormitories into colleges and universities, at the point when the engine had become exactly as cool as October?

XXIII. THE ONES WHO GOT PURPLE

135 PEARL, FRI. 12/20. MEAGHAN: THANX FOR
the rainbow beer. I wanted to give you my Pride beads
at the party, but was too shy. Can I see you without
your friends? 5169.

You would have been the first girl I guessed, I mean *kissed*, your
mouth surprising me by being just like a boy's mouth, as though
lips and tongues and teeth like ours were *human* rather than *girls'*,
surprising me so much that when I shut my eyes and slid my human lips and tongue around your peach and nectariney cunt, I
would have been surprised once more to put it all together: there
was nothing like this anywhere in the world of boys.

Fly-by could be a hot surprise on a cold night.

XXIV. WILD CARD

LYNETTE, YOUR UNIQUENESS HAS CAPTURED
my heart. You are "poetry" walking. I'm walking on air
and I'm ready to fly. I'd wing anywhere songward. For you.
I'd spread violets around your musical feet. 5199.

Lynette, your uniqueness. Wow. Whoa. I have to reckon with that
for a minute. *Lynette, your uniqueness has captured my heart.* That's different. That's uncut uplift. That's tap-dance, castanets, and pin-
wheels, with her name on it. Ticket to a Happy New Year. That's
an invitation to a magic-carpet ride, minus the maybe. There's
playing in the snow if I ever saw it, and I never did.

XXV. THE ONE WHO GOT AWAY

You: so beautiful, the people who served you at the coffee shop,
the bank, the photo shop, would have left voice-mail for you by the
time you got home from that round of errands, each message asking

you out on a date—and there would have been a little extra sugar, an error in your favor, and the photos would have clearly been "handled." Negatives would have been stolen.

They would not have made me jealous, the loops and loops of propositions from the delivery people, the receptionists, the human resources, the altar boys and girls, etc., for you would never have gone out with any of them, taken as you would have been with me, and only me, in your heart of hearts, to the point of not wanting me to worry, or even to waste any time wondering. Is what you would have said, year-in, year-out. But you would have been lying, as creepy little errors, not in my favor, would have slowly accrued to prove. I would not have known it was a revolving door.

Because the birds had not yet started to talk.

XXVI. THE ONE WHO GOT GOT

Me, You: Even if I had got you, you still would have gotten away.

XXVII. THE ONES WHO TOPSY-TURVY

CAROUSEL CAFE, TABLE BY THE RUBBER PLANT.
Girl you a cool suckah. I: dreads, new to the city. Let's go to the GH & dance a disco mile. Just friends. 5280.

Thanks, but friends I've already got. I've got dreads too. Winged, every last one.

XXVIII. THE ONE WHO GOT AWAY

Me: lying in bed on a midsummer Saturday, with big fat flies bruising up against the screen from time to time, until I couldn't tell where I left off and the cotton sheet began. Me: still longer lying still, 'til I could slow my very sorrow down. You: the object of the sorrow in the question: Where were you last night. The human-species chatter-through-the-ages question, one that falls from the tree in the fall of love, rotten, hollow, sere. Me: one ear to the world, hearing, for the first time ever, the birds. Suddenly each one had a call that could be transliterated from birdsong into English. In my yard that day, the birds made sense; they weren't saying tweet. Birdsong: *Cheater. Cheater. Cheater. Cheater.* Birdsong: *Additup. Additup. Additup.* Birdsong: *Read. Weepweep. Read. Weepweep.* I would get the message. I would follow the birds' advice and I would plunder your private things for the first time, and only then would I spy, in your computer, in your drawer, in the pocket of your pants, the notes, numbers, and wrappers, that overflowed the banks of: No, you wouldn't do that to Me: the cuckoo, female cuckold, me. But it would have been my own idea to clear out before noon, before I would ever have a chance to ask you: What the hell, before You: would have had to tell another lie. Or worse, the truth. If I had stuck around and asked, what might you not have said; what wouldn't you have told me: everything.

I had to make new floor plans suddenly. I more than moved house, I turned tail. I ran. I fled, did flee, but did not fly.

Birdsong: where You call that love and all my other questions would have gone.

XXIX. THE ONE WHO GOT AWEIGH

The round hole in the frozen surface of the lake. Saw you sink a line there. What you said about the sole, did you mean that? Want to go fishing for compliments?

XXX. QUIVER

Lynette, your uniqueness has captured my heart. Metrical, musical, *perfect*! Listen: ly-*nette*-your-u-*nique*-ness-has-*cap*-turedmy-*heart*. An iamb followed by three anapests. Or three anapests followed by an iamb. Either way: weak-strong-weak-weak-strong-weak-weak-strong-weak-weak-strong.

XXXI. DO YOU DO WAH DIDDY DIDDY DUM DIDDY DO?

Guano—a natural manure composed chiefly of the excrement of seabirds, valued as fertilizer:

Wanna chat; wanna hang; wanna hold your hand; wanna walk; wanna kiss; wanna drink; wanna dance; wanna talk; wanna go out; wanna stay in; wanna go for coffee or tea; wanna wanna go for me; wanna get married; wanna find another way; hey baby, wanna pull off those scabs and revel in the only itch that scratches itself?

XXXII. THE ONE WHO GOT AWAY

Maybe October had always been beautiful, the stealth weapon among months, unremembered in the face of snowfall, quiet against the noise of May and June, but coming around again, underdog in orange, gripping onto itself and the leaves. Maybe every year I had discovered it again as though for the first time. But you, with your cheek pressed against my hip last July, you would have shown me once and future Octobers still gripping. Untraceable months later, my skin would still have borne the imprint of your two tongues.

Hot and cold would have slid together as the me-and-you bird drove west in a brand-new two-tone Mantra.

XXXIII. GO AWAY

Me: marble arches. You: wax sundial. You: Up. Me: Down. Turnstile eternally between us.

XXXIV. PURPLE PROSE

Lynette, your uniqueness has captured my heart. Lovely tetrameter, hot damn. Who writes their ad in meter? 5199. Then there's the self-referential move (*You are "poetry" walking.*) in the next sentence delivered in delicate trimeter. See how the Lynette-seeking ad-placer brings down the stakes by alternating the meter, and then leaving off altogether, so as not to bonk Lynette over the head with it. Once having demonstrated its poetic sophistication, the ad humbles itself with references to popular courting tradition. The meter of the first couple of sentences is repeated in the next two. Then there's a break. Finally, the ad loops back to meter just by way of a little pun on "feet." Subtle enough, between the clichés, which sound, for some reason, sincere. There is, unaccountably, flight. Overall, this ad is as thoughtful as it is droll. I'm impressed.

XXXV. SAY YOU DO

There they go again, I say, then I see some new twists:

Wanna hold my hand; wanna watch for UFOs; wanna make love; wanna eat; wanna show me what you've got; wanna pump it up; wanna dance; wanna wake up tomorrow with me and pantomime breakfast; wanna self-amuse; wanna self-abuse while I watch; wanna fish for worms; wanna wiggle on over here, honey?

Then I hear a bird say: *Whynot. Whynot. Whynot.*

XXXVI. PURPLE HEARTS AND CLAY PIGEONS

You: giving blood, mobile-van courageous, horse-haired, cross-eyed, club-footed, thick-boned, red tee-shirt with a silver hubcap. Me: turned down on account of my history, horse-haired, star-crossed, club-weary, thick-tongued, and jealous of your golden blood or the phial it easily fills, or both.

XXXVII. THE LYNETTE LOVER

Could the Lover of Lynette just as well have said, *your particularities?* Yes, Lover could have. But it would have thrown off the meter. *Lynette, your particularities have captured my heart.* Not right.

Note that it is the *heart* and not the other organs that are captured in so many other clichés: the mind, the body, the imagination, the flag. Lover chooses the cliché purposefully, and above all, stays true to the meter. *Lynette, your uniqueness has captured my gizzard* doesn't scan with the same pizzazz.

XXXVIII. THE ONE WHO GOT AWAY

You would have shown me over the course of our years together how to use a compass, a slide rule, and, that time in the second-hand shop, an abacus. With a firm grasp of the mechanical as well as the metaphysical, not to mention the inside of my thighs, you would have tried to make it work with me. But for the greater good of the irreal. But for the mythical arrow that would have pierced the wordless bird right through the breast.

But I loved every finger on those calculating hands, the palms where I last saw my mind, the crook of the arm that held the head that used to house that mind, the ring of fire that rosied round the bed, the talk that took its time.

XXXIX. THE ONES WHO WERE BLUE

Sometimes things change suddenly. Like when birds talk. And in that split second, there is no place safe from the overwhelming, all-destroying cobalt-cold river of rushing platelets with the blanket force of death. Zillions of slivered discs, platinum, overrunning the banks, while under the thunder, a little bird shrieks an alarm, heartfelt if reedy, to all creatures still capable of flight: *Make for the only remaining havens, those high off the ground, do it now. Leave speed in the dust, now, now in your haste.* It says *now*, it squeaks *NOW*, it insists, the warning pitched so high it shatters even the satyr's sopranino flute, urgently, urgently: *TREEEEE!!!!!* And again: *TREEEEE!!!!!*

Then, in the middle of July, the sprightly kobold heads for the hills.

XL. THE ONES WHO GOT AWAY SCOT FREEEEE!!!!!

The rare Lynette bird takes a turn on the Ferris wheel. The bucket, empty but for a pair of mittens, still warm, swings on its unoiled hinges, singing *Getoverit. Getoverit.*

XLI. THE LYNETTE BIRD

Lynette, your uniqueness has captured my heart. Of all of Lynette's qualities, it is her uniqueness that has captured her admirer's heart. So Lynette is unique, is she? That would mean she is "one of a kind." So I could not be the same kind of person as Lynette. But if we are both designated female, do we not share this attribute in some way? Are we not then of the same kind? And among, say *women* (just picking a random category here, okay perhaps not random, among infinite others that could work in this investigation into Lynette), must we not necessarily represent different particular individual possibilities, different kinds of women? Yes, we must. Could it then really be said that Lynette is more unique among women than I? That's like saying one totality is more complete than another; by definition, it cannot be true. One thing, or one woman in this case, cannot be more unique than another. And nothing, or no one, can be superlatively unique, any more than she can be relatively unique, as I was instructed when I attempted to argue to argumentative friends that the artichoke is the most unique vegetable. Remember that, oh Lover-of-Lynette. I cannot logically be less than every bit as unique as Lynette, though I am, no doubt, a different kind of rara avis. For example, I could be more responsive to advertising, metered verse, and mystery than Lynette. You never know.

XLII. MONIQUE FROM WAITSVILLE

> IN MUDDY'S AROUND 9:30 ON 3/16. JUST
> in from the rain in rubber boots. Your friend had
> purple hair. Acorn salt-and-pepper shakers on
> my lazy Susan. Wanna talk over coffee? 1003.

Just how much can you say about coffee?

I can't say I smell spring coming, but I can say I'll step lightly as a dragonfly on the first of every frozen month until the thick ice is puckered first, then thin, then gone. Sometimes things change slowly; the fire in the sky burns three more minutes into each successive day.

XLIII. ME AND WHO

Sometimes I want to call that 5199—not stop, not pass go, run, don't walk, quick quick, call the number of the one whose ad has caught my fancy—could it be the number of my dreams? Or get a number of my own and write right back: Lover, your advert has captured my eye. But no, because precisely what's good about 5199 is there's only one Lynette worth waxing so lyrical about. I hope she reads *I Spy*.

Maybe the dirt will turn up green in this new year and birds will do what birds should do. Hop down to earth once in a light-blue while. Fly-by no more.

Let Lynette get lucky, let the compass tail of the dragonfly point true north for her, to spring. And let the buzz of bees be what it is, a harbinger of spring spread wide. Let flowers be followed by fruit. Why not?

XLIV. SINGING ARROW

You: 5199. Me: Not Lynette, as least not yet.

XLV. AND/OR BETTER YET

Let her have 5199 and let some as yet unsung rain of whirligigs, some shower of sporangiospore, some spectral spray of future come and purple-fruit my hopes. Yet like Lynette, I'd like to be not one of many—one of one of one. Until then, I'll ramp on and up another day and night and April down the mountain in my way.

XLVI. ROYAL FLUSH

If I had, or if I do, and if you would or if you will, and if we really had, or one day have to have and get, oh full-on raging orange corpuscular joy. Stars come uncrossed. Dreams come unscrewed, unsprung, far-flung. Fantasy is mist; it hangs invisibly blue in the air but we really do get wet. And the Ferris wheel hums and the bird of petrifaction in the TREEEEE!!!!! falls to the ground in two clay pieces, violet traces of the path of the arrow grooved into each piece, and the me-and-you bird falls silent. The Lynette bird winks her green diamond eye.

ELENA = AGAIN

N OUESU BUT. N OUESU BUT EAR OUESU BUT.

_ _____ ___. _ _____ ___ ___ _____ ___.

N BESU OUCK BUT ISUT EAR ISUT EAR AIQ

_ ____ ____ ___ ____ ___ ____ ___ ___

N'X LINAL KI OUESU ELENA. N'X WI WITTH

_'_ _____ __ _____ _____. _'_ __ _____

UOUAE. N RIA'K QEAK KI BGTK HIG, FGK N

_____. _ ___'_ ____ _____ ___,___ _

EX; BUTU N EX OUESNAL HIG BGTKNAL ELENA.

__; ____ _ __ _____ ___ _____ _____.

45

Round-Trip Blues

October, 1990: Where I Live Now

The kids across the street spend a hell of a lot of time running around after each other in circles. The bush outside my window is a bit greener nowadays, since it rained, but it will be light until a little less late than yesterday. This evening, the little girl across the street is wearing a dress, for the first time, a maroon velvet dress, very pretty. It's Friday. It's early evening, like it is every day in the early evening. One seventh of the time, it's Friday. My desk overlooks the street and I sit studying hour after hour. I moved here to study drama and I do it all day: I read plays, I watch them play. The kids across the street—a little girl and her big brother—are married as only a brother and sister can be, as married as I was to my big brother. The little girl is becoming a girl. Tonight is the dress rehearsal.

Mark and I babbled to each other in sounds that we knew weren't even morphemes and called it French. We faced each other, cocked our heads to opposite sides, and pushed our necks up against each other's, combined into a strange new animal, push-me-pull-you, Siamese white kids. *Look, Mom*, we called to her, *we're necking*. We borrowed her red plastic price counter, hijacked its boring supermarket purpose to count cars going by on our local Broadway. We shared a horror at the discovery that the name Broadway made many people think of a street in New York. We got a book called *We Came in Peace* at the gas station. It had pictures from the moon, and all the words the astronauts said when they

47

first landed on it. Mark and I turned two straw-seated dining-room chairs on their backs on his bed. We sat upside down in the chairs, ignoring the ceiling, facing outer space, and read the astronauts' words from the book.

This evening, maybe because of her dress, the little girl can't quite catch up with her brother, so she trails behind him in the leaves, carrying two Dixie cups, and trailed in turn by a loop of limp string.

Wait a minute, this is California. Why are the leaves falling?

November, 1990: Where I Lived Then

From one coast to another. Direct, non-stop, one-way, round-trip.

Grandma is slowly, dearly, departing. I have come home to say goodbye, so it is no surprise I dreamed that there was a graveyard outside my window, under the big old tree, that it had been there all along, but I had never noticed it until...more people started dying. Suddenly, my grandmother isn't the only one going wherever she's going. It's gay men, by the thousands, some nuns in Central America, and Robert Alton Harris, the first man executed in California in twenty-five years (so some things *do* change there, or do they just return in more and less attenuated periodicities?). Inspired by a pick-up truck with a sign all over its back that said, *Now we are all killers*, I wasted $9.95 on a telegram telling Governor Wilson I think capital punishment is inhumane. And it isn't just people, either. Roadkill, pets, endangered species. Outside the window, where the graveyard was in the dream, by that knee of root, isn't that where Mark and I buried the bat that flew unwanted into the house, that flapped our mother, that our dad—suburban spelunker only missing the pith helmet—had to trap in a milk carton with a tennis racket. Then our dad had to close the carton quickly and shake, stunning the bat on the slick cardboard walls to what end. And it isn't just animals too. Cities, languages. Piles upon piles of cars. Is death just now beginning to accelerate, or am I just beginning to notice? Have I been asleep this whole time. This weekend, anyway, I revive my old tricks; I pretend to sleep, because my parents' home encases the nuclear material that is two grown-up children and their estranged forebears.

Guildenstern says, *Death's death, isn't it?* Of course it is, but that's not the whole answer. Death is death, no question, but it's not the only thing that is.

I can't stop looking back. I loop back to earlier times, to other firsts. I still remember the weak winter light out the window when I first chose someone to love, after I got out of this suburban lockbox. Here was freshman year. But where were those famously carefree college days, which only shrunk toward winter? Here were dormitoria: the fake hot air inside, recycled smell of youth and books year-in year-out of the same ventilation ducts. Here was someone with an open-handed interest in the original Elektra, someone who couldn't see the relation that contracted me along with the light as Christmas vacation approached. I think of the small peace there was in being loved, and the always larger sadness in being unable to love back. Branches, kisses, despair, disbelief in spring.

New England with no leaves on the trees, with the dirt packed hard from months of being frozen, hard and brown; the buildings around the yard were warmer than the ground—New England was sad and cold. All the people I met there were cold. Even my first lover could not keep me warm. Trees are like people, them and me: cold and sad. A tree standing alone in a wide open yard like that lonely campus, in the cold winter, standing on cold ground—such a tree is always sad, whether trees have feelings or not, because I was or am that tree, or I thought I was like that tree, or I think like that tree, and am sad. Such a tree spreads its leafless fingers wide, signing apartness, crowded apartness.

December, 1990: Where I Live Now

Framed by my study break: the arboreal dispute resolution professional points her finger up at the problem, while a mercenary tree killer watches and licks his chops. A semi-circle of kids cranes its collective neck trying to see. Apparently, the neighbors have disagreed, but I have never seen them do it. Small homeowners are concerned, maybe for the safety of their small homes, maybe because they can't afford larger yet and life is short. One must have won; the tree will be cut back. Specifically, the killer will remove a sagging horizontal branch that seems to threaten the side addition of the bungalow next door. Leaves fall from that tree, which isn't normal here, which may therefore be a sign of some sickness, from which a professional might have inferred some threat to its structural integrity, or maybe this is the subtle look of seasonal change in California. I will not ask. Soon it will begin raining and never stop. I only know that it has been the yellow time of year, which followed the brown, which is what became of the green, I'm told, over the course of months. Someone tells me the rain will bring the green back and I believe it. The bush is greener already.

California-style cold is not so cold. Strange, like rain, it seems to slow the traffic down, impede the people who don't know from real cold, from snow. It is only cool. But it is gray. Easy and vacuous thoughts, like the heat, have risen. This cool shakes me down, leaves me alone with the desk and the chair, the things that cling, as though we matter mattered. My first semester in graduate school here was warm (and hot—I went through a couple of lovers) and it went like steam. Went away. I have tried to resume my studies, to pick it all back up again after Thanksgiving: drama, drama criticism. Criticism. But my memory keeps flicking back to that first semester in college, as though for a comparison. Around this time that year, I first tried to love someone; it was warm and hot and it convected—before it vaporized altogether. Then and there I swore off love and marriage, those lose-lose institutions. Whether one goes, while one stays put—or not—whoever's left is hacking away at the stump for years. This time around, I'm staying away from both.

January, 1991: Where I Lived Then

Tree removal is death after death—it makes air where there used to be tree. Vectors are two dimensional and so are imaginary; like them, tree branches have those two dimensions—motion, direction—but immeasurably more, they have a third. The cylinder which is the trunk of the tree does not just denote volume, it *is* volume. Though its branches are petrified and its trunk rotting through, the tree, I mean its presence now, is not a conclusion at which we arrive—no, along with the termites and the birds and squirrels, we make our real home in the brittle wood.

Is this a Christmas vacation? Again, this is a Christmas vacation. Do I have double vision: out west, they brought down a branch—back here, the whole tree has come down, at just the time of year when evergreens are felled by millions, for twenty dollars or for joy, depending on which side of the transaction you stand. Mark says our father killed it; he wants me to agree so badly, he comes at me with an ancient gesture, aiming at my neck, but this time, to shake me. No, I am a grown-up. Do I have double vision or am I seeing things where things are not? Yes, I am. The cut-rate tree removers botched the job and left a stump where an absence should be.

In her last moments of vigor, in this, her unaccountable second wind, Grandma goes out to her final stomping ground and hacks with a small spade at the enormous stump, hack, hack, each cold dawn tick-tocked by futility. If she could feel her hands, they'd be frozen. Lodged in the woody knobs here where she kneels, the fourth dimension of the tree, present like the past. Likewise, over her head, the air where the tree used to wave and crack holds the memory of earlier winds suddenly, unevenly, upsetting an infinity of leaves, the myriad sometimes summery memories of shifting and patchy green shade.

February, 1991: Where I Live Now

The Persian Gulf Crisis, which followed toe-poking at braggadaccio-drawn lines in the sand, has now yielded to a Gulf War. TV tells me so. I watch a show on the domestic effects of the war, meaning those felt in the United States; leading the pack is the rupture of families by the imminent war. Never mind the rupture of Iraqi families, or the blood on all of our hands because of it. Pictured on my TV screen is a living room in which a white mother in South Carolina and her two very young daughters are watching their own TV screen, and on *their* screen is the husband/daddy at the front. He is saying that he loves them and misses them. One of the daughters is hugging the TV saying, *Daddy, I'm going to get a mermaid. Daddy, I'm going to get a mermaid.* The other daughter starts out watching the video of her father, but shortly throws herself into her mother's arms, wailing. I disbelieve the crying daughter, or rather, disbelieve what the story wants me to believe, that she is crying over the absence of her father. I insist that she is upset because her mother and the TV camera and the TV people in her living room have told her that she is upset. She is crying because she believes them or because she is upset at the upset caused by their presence in her home, or because she doesn't want to be told what to feel. *No*, I say to the person who is watching with me, *they're not upset about their father leaving*. There's no difference. I mean, he's not there when he's there and he's not there when he's not there, so there's no difference—even in the best of cases. The person watching with me scoffs at me; when he was a boy, his father killed himself. We have a difference of opinion. I ask him if he thinks that it universally makes a difference when a father leaves—no matter when or where—and he says yes. No. Only in the cases where it means an end to getting whacked.

I never see a mother on this block. I see no fathers, especially not the one next door, and also no mothers. But when I sit stock still, looking up from the page and into the middle distance, I think I hear the creaking wheels of the shopping carts the mothers maneuver up and down the aisles of the grocery stores, wearing deeper the grooves in the frozen linoleum, and I hear them standing behind heaps of goods piled hari-kari in the carts, waiting in the checkout line, screaming. Into the vacuum-packed Dixie cup at the other end of my string.

March, 1991: Where I Lived Then

Grandma would be sick for three acts. She would die in the fourth. In the fifth, I will manifest my guilt, which is unrelated to my grandmother, unless my father and my brother count. I loved them both; I would not side with one. Just like a girl.

I would come home for the funeral. It would be nothing new.

All the violence takes, and/or took, place off-stage. I never once saw red running blood. I've seen purple yield to blue then green then yellow, so the blood must come and go, but the skin of the body the tree the carton the house holds it in; the curtain works, and what hurts occurs between scenes.

April, 1991: Where I Live Now

I hear the father come home next door. He is slamming mad, comes in yelling, just as I hear him wake up every morning yelling. Because I have no window on the side, I have never seen this father or the child he yells at every day. Sometimes I see the taillights of his car when he goes out at night, and in an instant, the carbon monoxide blows by. I have never heard the voice of a woman from that side. I stop reading, my body tenses. It is anybody's father coming down the hall yelling. I can't read for the same reason Mark couldn't sleep when he came home for Christmas, even though he is now an adult: father's footsteps in the house. Is he mad, is he coming to get me? The kid starts yelling back, just as I hear him wake up every morning yelling back. If I were the kid, I think I would not yell back but try to do everything right, find the right thing to say, anything to stop the yelling. I wait for the voices to escalate; the voices escalate. I wait for the father to hit the child. There I am looking up from my book, waiting for the voices in another house to reach such a pitch that only violence could follow. I'm waiting, but something's missing. I am actually disappointed because I don't hear the whacking and the crying that ought to follow the yelling voices.

For school, I am reading a theory that the gasp in the movie audience when a car blows up expresses not fright, shock, or pity, but the gratified expectation of destruction, lovely, come true, before their eyes. Narrative at its sweetest: closure. Yes, I think so, but to be one of the audience and to know why you gasp....

Meanwhile, the war ends, or seems to end, with a whimper.

My father came, my father went. When he went, I pulled his shirt out of its hiding place and smelled him in it less and less each time. When he came, he yelled at his own miniature, for being his own miniature. *Mama's boy*, he called him—how horrifyingly unoriginal—*Mama's boy*. When at seventeen, Mark had had it and took his own turn leaving, he asked me to come with him. He more than asked. He said, *If you stay, you're siding with him. It means you think our father was right to do what he did.* He said that after he left, my father would do to me what he had used to do to Mark. I always thought he would; I always knew he wouldn't. Both. Afterwards, my father said Kaddish for my brother, which was merely symbolic, and melodramatic at that. I stood by. Until Grandma was sick, not merely sick, but dying, but not dead, Mark didn't speak a word to me. When we were both at home at the same time, like this winter, it was taciturn civil war on the second floor, only more domestic: divorce.

I am reading *Acte Sans Parole*. It reminds me of the time I called Mark and listened to the fiber-optic air where he wouldn't say my name, where he didn't have to repeat that it was an act of betrayal when I stayed. It reminds me of Robert Alton Harris and his death-row mates, who are scared all over again.

May, 1991: Where I Lived Then

The staged reading of the will. The declaiming of my Grandma's will. The distribution of her petty property. Mark is not on hand, nor is he mentioned. I am inheriting $1,250, twice the cost of the ticket. Now I can buy my own price counter.

I dream that I am married to my brother and I keep getting the laundry and the garbage mixed up and I will cook dinner for him and his girlfriend every night because they can't because their nine-to-five jobs make it impossible, whereas a student's schedule is so flexible that I will have time to cook dinner.

June, 1991: Where I Live Now

Driving past the military cemetery in Colma, I see stones all of a single size and shape, so that the center is always where I am—moving—and all the stones swim, suddenly synchronized, into radial alignment from the point which is my eyes and is moving. Not accelerating, I move at a constant speed and so, constantly, and at a constant speed, do the thousands of stones, of a single size and shape, form radii, constantly shifting radii, radiating out from a constantly shifting center—me—neat like ranks of cooperating dots and aisles clearing forth. Orderly. Dead.

Do wars end, or do they come around again? Those troops over there, were they torn between shrinking from enemies and wielding unbeatable arms? And now, are they just pretending to sleep; it's a hell of a maneuver to perform for the rest of time.

Last night I woke up in the middle of the night and uttered the longest litany of anxieties, driving myself and the other person in bed almost crazy. Repetition, deferral, trinities, Professor Cole, Professor Cole, Professor Kahn, Jean and Alan, assignments, appointments, pencils and pens, Building 20, Building 30, Building 40, Building 50, awards office, bursar's office, registrar, financial aid, trucks, bridges, buildings, buildings, buildings, buildings, books, books, books, books, repetition, fragmentation, diachronic designation, modernism, post-modernism, the historicizing tendency of narration, 2:05, oh my god, oh my god, it's so late, so early, so late...repetition...repetition...deferral....

July, 1991: Where I Lived Then

I'm out of time, out of place, confused. Time after time I come back to this place—I don't know how not to live here. Time goes by, I go other places, I even go to California, and this place remains here without me in it. The periodic audaciousness of it. What do twenty years mean to the bricks in the sidewalk—maybe centimeters askew where the root of a tree has pushed up. What do twenty years mean to me?

I'm dissipated into days and minutes all under this same cold gray sky, with roots coming up between the bricks in the sidewalk in the peripheral vision of my whole life. I'm sad and cold and so tired. So. I could be cold on either coast on a gray July day, and I could be tired for twenty years. I could be both tired and asleep, living and dying. Waking, no walking, on the street, I hardly notice, but I do, it's normal to me here. Normal.

Of course these thoughts bore me by now. The fantasy of having once been warm, cozy, and light, inside on a cold, cloudy day exactly like this five years ago. The thought of people I'd like to love. Friends of mine, back out west, who may never know I can't. A freshman year that never was. The continuous absence. The missing what I never had. The many times I wouldn't have minded being dead. Instead, death keeps happening to everyone and everything else. I just keep getting older. I've grown up but not out of it.

I dreamed my father died in a huge explosion. In successively closer mushroom eruptions, flame and smoke consumed everything. Black smoke came close and closer and too close to choking me, who watched, until it seemed he must be dead. And yet I could not believe it, could only insist on proliferating, with irrational logic, arguments about how he could possibly have stayed alive through the combustion. It was impossible to imagine that the ashen landscape had swallowed him up, that I would not be seeing him again.

It's very important not to try to understand what two weeks is. Try to remember that it is a spring break. Students have fun. I am a student, studying to be more than a granddaughter, more than a daughter, more than a sister, goddamn it. I may be, I may be, someday I may be a lover. I will I will I will not ever be a wife. I repeat, I will not.

August, 1991: Where I Live Now

The brother knows that between the two of them they can figure out and accomplish more than twice as much as either one of them can alone. He appears, today, to consult the little girl regarding the dispensation of a mysterious object in his hands. They deliberate, she appears to speak, and then appears done speaking. He appears to nod in grave agreement as to the course of action she has outlined. But he will need her help. Brothers and sisters must have had different relationships in former times. You might think that any man, in any historical period, who had grown up with a sister would know that women are not inferior to men, but obviously that isn't true. Think how early little boys must be taught to turn on their own sisters.

They cross the street toward me. Solemnly, they place the object on the ground under the scar at the crook of our common neighbors' tree.

For some reason, I knew I was going to die. My mother was there and I had a little sister. We were in a place like a morgue: there were big steel drawers. I told my little sister to look away and then opened a drawer; it had three dead bodies in it that looked like huge fish skeletons—one long spine-like bone, and bits of flesh, without even skin—no recognizable human features. My mother asked why I wanted to look at it. I said, *In a way, it's very beautiful; among the many other things I am, I am also flesh and bones.* How to explain that my arms and my legs are still on that bed, waving in space. I put my face against her and cried; she disappeared into a curtain, whose velvet absorbed my tears.

Maybe I had been sentenced to die, maybe I was waiting upstairs knowing it would be soon—or no—I must have been downstairs because the front door kept coming unbolted. Then I knew someone had broken in because the woman downstairs screamed. I had a cup of tea in one hand and a pen in the other, thought I would pour hot tea on the perpetrator, and woke up.

It was Mr. Death and Mark rolled into one, breaking into my house. That, or the person next to me in bed rolled over, poked me unconsciously, and broke into my dreams, provoking another nightmare.

Last year I wrote that tree removal was death and this year I don't think so any more. This year I think it's very important to distinguish between reality and figures of speech, which is to say, between figures of speech. Tree removal is a metaphor for death— no, death is a metaphor for tree removal. Not just a metaphor. You can't restage a tree.

Next time around, Daddy, I'm going to get a mermaid. Swim up and down with her like a sine wave in the blue medium, waterproof and happy.

September, 1991: Where I Live Now

It's fall. Today was not blue. The tree outside my window is turning yellow—but not because it's fall because that doesn't happen in California. It's not losing any leaves so it must be dying. It's the converse of the lesson I learned last year about the difference between death and the change of seasons in the suburbs.

It's impossible to imagine that another year, another decade, another generation will not brink us to another showdown shown on TV, giving on to another crisis, followed by another war. *When* is just a question of the attenuation of the period. Does death occur or recur—yes, in every arena, every time. If only the soldiers would study with the astronauts, come in peace, go into, and out of, orbit rather than battle, save the advances for technology, and go home when the Tang runs out. But since time immemorial, or at least since the dawning of Western drama, civilians don uniforms, however unwittingly, and walk straight into the traps the playwrights would seem to want to spare us—for example, the literature seems to recommend against endogamy—but never do. The show must go on.

Another kid on the block learned how to ride a bike yesterday. The day before, all the children ganged up on the newspaper delivery boy. They were shooting rubber bands at him, and he swung his fist at them, his wide canvas bag full of papers swinging right behind it, the bag thumping his back as it reached the end of its short tether. Today was, I should say *is*, merely cool and sad.

Blond children go rolling by the window in yet another toy with wheels—this time, a little wagon. It is cool and gray; there are rosy little blooms in their little white cheeks. They are not cute, but they are a little funny. Another cat chases another squirrel up a tree. Incredible, flat repetition, windowed. These are not events in the suburbs, they are its characteristics in perpetual motion.

Potatoes, You Ask

Madly. More madly. Potatoes. More madly than that.
Fiendishly. Perpetually. Like a thing possessed.

I say these are adverbs qualifying the verb *to write*.
Potatoes, you ask.

all kinds of people on the Q train

rattling horizontal in the subway car, one gazes one dozes another drifts off, but the junkie always nods. nods on the subway nods in the waiting room nods at the wheel of the car, and nods at home with the television up too loud to think while a child pulls at her sleeve, *mommy wake up, i'm hungry*. but it's always a waiting room wherever she is, and she's always nodding. off.

we rattling along we know the nods. it's not a nap.

the camel coat on my right elbows the high heels to *his* right silently to say, look at the child. the child breathes on the window blacked by the racing headlong flashlight tunnel walls and draws an O in the greasy condensation of her breath.

some like it nap some like it nod. the child turns to her mother slumping like some cilium in a lung, turns away, and says to the graffiti above her head, *let's pretend we're in a spaceship*.

we know, honey, we've nodded too or seen it done a hundred thousand million times ourselves. several bags across the aisle leans over asking, *is your mother sick*. *no she's not sick, she's tired*, says the child, says it first to several bags, and then says to the X crossed on the pentimentoed O, *and she's not my mother*. train *ch-ch ch-ch*.

cilia protect inside from germs by waving them away, by waving wave-like, and also usher eggs down fallopian tubes, beating, beating rhythmic-like. cilia sleep when the poison hits, and later on they die.

we woke us up, we'd wake you up, we red-haired, ham-handed, head-setted, barging on barging off, brief-cased, and even we begging passengers, but before that, at least one of we was nodding just like you were dropping through unmemory of heavy-headed years.

the child looks at *AVISO*, what to do for help, says to the ad for quitting, *let's pretend the train's on fire.*

the train *IS* on fire—honey, we're here to say so. the car explodes into daylight east off canal street, tube without a tube the sun scream whistles, the chorus gets up, beats our drums and waves our arms, our flagella flailing:

shake off the junk. shock-shock your cilia into consciousness. cilia: jump back up junk off. see with your ear to the ground the subway underneath it see the cars crash out of the tunnel. under our asses the rattling rails rise over chinatown four five six seven stories high. get off your ass. rise above bazaar below. cilia: unbend. cilia: see the beautiful raggedy-ass subway cars holding iron hands and hurtling single file over the neighboring rails back at us westward over the bridge from brooklyn. cilia: see the characters down there prattling in the morning air singing to the people: food, food, food, and jewels, and reasons to come buy and reasons to come off the junk, and cilia: smell the iron smell the dumplings and kumquats rampling down below, and cilia: see the tugboats on the river and the red lights at the tops of cranes to warn the planes and at the piers to warn the boats. come unhigh. naps and braids and snapping gum and golden chains and shiny heads are gazing, dozing, drifting off, while all we open eyes are pulling for the tugboat, singing: shake your junky cilia. junkie: you: get up and dance. throw off the clotted i can't get off it.

only junkies nod. it's not a nap, we shriek and sway. snap out of it.

well we might wave, but you're the arm she pulls on when she's hungry, and if you'd only lift your head you'd have fed her even in the tunnels out of which we've come and into which we now go hurtling bridge gone by light change to green to yellow red to warn the trains to station stop and go and hurry *mommy isn't this our stop. shouldn't we get off here mommy isn't this our—*

B. & G. & I

B. was the eldest of three children, disliked butter, liked Swedish films, and had been captain of the debate club in his high school. B.'s fifth toe on both feet pointed outwards, at odds with the rest of the pack. I flushed cold when I first saw this, not because such a deformity would give me even a shiver of unease, but because of the uncanny staring straight at both sides of me. G.'s fifth toes turned outward too. G. too was the eldest of three children, disliked butter, and liked Swedish films. And G. had also been captain of the debate club in her high school. Not like butter, preposterous. Trained to argue, disastrous for the lover torn between them. With all that in common, weird and eerie.

After a while, the torn routine began to fray all three of our nerves, so we got together at my place to discuss the situation. We were too young to know better—our three ages combined didn't even add up to an average human lifespan in these United States. B. and G. sat on the couch, a photo of him on the endtable at her left and a photo of her on the wall behind his right shoulder, their four faces arrayed like a panel of judges. As I sat in my easy chair facing them, I could see that if they ganged up on me, I would be outnumbered, but they were in no mood to forge an alliance.

"I get to keep her because I had her first," G. said to B.

"I was just going to say the same thing!" said B. They looked at me.

"I know, I know," I proposed, "I'll split myself in two and you can each have half."

B. and G. practically spit. They consulted the paper quickly and quickly left the apartment so they could catch the beginning of some dreary interminable angst-fest with subtitles. It was time for a little comic relief, I guess; this was the one thing they could agree on—this, and that they hated each other.

The truth is, G. did have me first, but B. didn't know it. Just because you bare your feet to me doesn't mean I'm going to tell you everyone I'm sleeping with. That's my philosophy. Anyway, it was irrelevant. I couldn't bear to live without the full weight of both contempts, his and hers. His and her monogrammed contempts, B. and G. Then there was me, liking butter, very much disliking Swedish films, and as you can see, unable to weigh the pros and cons judiciously. On top of which—and I saw this as a matter of personal shame at the time, because it was so obvious, so overdetermined—I was an only child. However, I was not ashamed to admit that I had two lovers at the same time because that indicated to me how very very cute I must have been in my disarray, which indicates to you how very very very young I was.

I had met G. at an ACT OUT rally. Even in that context, we were somewhat marginalized by our unusual values. See, G. and I shared a political fetish. We agreed that the greatest oppression of all is one that hardly anybody seems to notice—the social requirement that people couple up, pair off, live and love in units of two. Marriage? What is marriage such that it should be the only real option available? We called it the Tyranny of the Dyad, and if we could not bring it to its knees double-footedly, we could at least model alternatives. G. was as engaged as the day is long, and just as engaging too, hair and eyes blazing with white heat. And I'll give her credit: G. was willing to try to put our utopian fantasies to the test, to try to make our triangular thing work. Theoretically. Some days.

B. was a theater critic, emphasis on *critic*, whose weekly column in the local paper was two parts sarcasm to one part earnest hope for a better future for theater. To put it another way, he never had anything good to say, which made him a frightening figure for those of us who worked in the theater. I met him through a friend of a friend at a party and from his first sneer at me, I was hooked. B.'s was the best-looking sneer I had ever seen and when it spoke it issued the wittiest, witheringest send-up of the play I had just finished working on. Imagine the Three Stooges as spies sent to infiltrate Los Alamos during the war, and you get an idea of what the play was about. Which is to say that the show was, from the outset, generically challenged; mixing comedy and tragedy is a risky business, and it almost never comes out as well on stage as it does in real life. Perhaps aspiring to do a better job of it myself, I was drawn into the arms of B.'s unending review. So when he said, "This party sucks, do you want come home with me?" I said yes. Unbeknownst to me, at the time, B. had a girlfriend already, or had previously had her and came to have her again soon thereafter, I've never been clear on which. I guess that's why he was willing to entertain my double dealings. But what did become clear, after a few months in which B. and I found ourselves strangely compatible, was that the other girlfriend had opted out of the square dance. In so doing, she pulled the fourth leg out from under us.

Beyond their taste in food and entertainment, beyond their penchant for disagreeing with the whole world, there was one other thing B. and G. had in common, but only on those days when G. could not bring her personal feelings and her political views into alignment: they both wanted me to choose between the two of them. In fact, they both wanted to be the chosen one. It was like being dehydrated and trying to choose between oxygen and hydrogen. I absolutely could not decide. The only thing I could decide was to seek the help of a psychotherapist. "Hallelujah, yes, good idea, excellent idea, and not a moment too soon," G. said, heaving the sigh of the ages. "Oh great," scoffed B., rolling his eyes heavenward. I think he was afraid the next step would be couples therapy, or maybe triples therapy. I got the names and numbers of three practitioners in town from G.'s ex-girlfriend, who was herself in the profession.

The first therapist never returned my call. The second therapist called back immediately, to say he didn't have an opening until the following month. I made an appointment for the next month. I didn't see how we could all go on even a few days longer the way we had been doing, but I could always cancel the appointment if we achieved any resolution. On the other hand, we had already been going on this way for a year and a half. For an untenable situation, it was phenomenally stable.

The third therapist had a slot open the next day—what luck. It only took me one sentence to tell her about my basic predicament. "I've got two lovers and we're all unhappy about it."

"What do you do for work?" she asked. "Do you have a job?" *Very astute*, I thought. I was, in fact, between jobs, unemployed you might say, and I was impressed that she had managed to derive this from a single sentence. *Interesting angle*, I thought. *I should throw myself into something outside myself, and outside our love triangle, do something useful in the world, forget about B. and G. eight hours a day, if not drop both of them altogether.*

"Nothing," I responded. "And no, not at the moment."

"Then how do you plan to pay for treatment?" she wanted to know. "If you're not covered by insurance, I can't see you."

"In other words," said G., when I told her how the session had gone, "she can't see you."

"Well, those are exactly the same words," I pointed out. "But yeah, no."

A month later, I went to the second therapist. He claimed to want to know about my early childhood, because, although he could of course only speak preliminarily, my situation sounded so "Mommy, Daddy, me." I would have asked if that were a technical term, but I couldn't get a foot in the door of all the precocious diagnosis: "Symmetry... stability... baby makes three...." He made me feel like crying so I didn't go back.

To prove that I had no issue with them, I confided in my parents. "Aiiee," my mother cried, "what did we do to make you so fucked up?" My father laughed until the tears ran down to his upturned hands. "And the problem is?" he finally coughed out.

Self-help classes? Spiritual guidance? Clarifying diet? Where could I turn, what could I do? Quit drinking? Just joking.

My cash supply was dwindling. Suddenly, dropping out of the flyspace, a job offer, short-term, three months on tour doing tech work for a theater group I had worked with once before. It wasn't exactly a job, but there was a nominal stipend and it got me out of town. I might as well not have bothered to go. My cell phone swallowed the distance as I logged up the telephone hours—late-night calls to G., early-morning calls to B., guilty sleep in between. Three months later, my debt was greater than my intake had been. At the end of the gig, I had to lie to both of them; I said I would be returning home on Wednesday, and then surprised B. by seeming to come home early on Monday, and then surprised G. by showing up at her place early, on Tuesday. It was the only trick I could think of to avoid a scene where I would have to choose which one would come to meet me at the train station, and which one to wound—or worse, they would both come.

G. wanted to talk about it all a lot more. I didn't want to—a lot. We had to talk a lot about whether to talk about it a lot. I said, "We've already talked ourselves a whole Swedish screenplay, only unfortunately, I understood the words. Now you want to start on a sequel." G. pointed out that while we had indeed talked a great deal, we had never really gotten down to the core of the problem, which, she now postulated, was my fear of commitment. I had to laugh. I did, too hard. "Oh no," I cried, "you know that's not it, you know that my worst fear is losing you. Either of you! You know I'd commit to you both in a heartbeat. I'd co-co-habit, like indefinitely, if only you guys would agree."

G. had no fear of commitment, especially not to her own ideas: "I just think maybe we should talk about it." She pushed her hair away from her face.

"I don't want to, and you can't make me, so I win!" I trumped, but how could I really be proud of the victory?

"Well then," G. said, "give me a foot massage, it's the least you can do." Ultimately, I had to accede to her argument, and sometimes, frankly, I preferred her funky fifth toes to her funky feelings, so I massaged her feet, thinking I'd gotten away with something.

B. didn't want to talk; now he wanted to get married. Over breakfast one morning, this: "You know, honey, I've been thinking, maybe we should get married…. Maybe even before my little sister's wedding next winter." He smiled his sideways smile.

I was astounded; had he not heard any of my many lengthy speeches on the topic, or had he simply not believed them? "Hi," I wanted to say, "Have we met before? My name is No Fucking Way In Hell, Ever." I was stupid enough that I thought that he thought it was a relief, and sexy to boot, that I would never want to get married. Wrong. It was me who thought that. Who knows what he thought; he seemed like a stranger sometimes. What I did say was, "Here, have some butter, darling."

How slippery the slope between respect and disdain—theirs for me and mine for them. As B. and G. catalogued my moral, psychological, and political failures, I see-sawed, back and forth. Sometimes I thought, *They're right. I'm a coward, a waffler, a bad ad for bisexuality.* Other times I questioned their righteousness, in addition to questioning their taste. If they didn't like me so much and if they didn't like the situation, why were they sticking around? I was cute, but I wasn't irresistible; there had to be something in it for them. Complaint and desire are the flip sides of the same coin, and that coin was our common currency, B.'s and G.'s and mine. Obviously, I craved the judgment they found so gratifying to lavish on me. And if I was also irritated by their appraisal, I was more terrified of living without either one of them. But I also didn't want to make them miserable every day of all of our lives. After all—or haven't I mentioned this?—I loved them. I just wanted them to go on making me miserable forever. How fine the line between love and misery.

I meditated…for about a minute. I unplugged my phone… for about two minutes. I consulted a psychic. He said, "Get a job." And that was before I paid him in nickels and dimes, so I knew he had the gift. I read the want ads every morning and I searched the web every afternoon. I pounded the proverbial pavement into the ground.

Bordering on desperate, I called my college drama teacher and asked if she had any idea where I could find some work. It had not been so very long since I had run the gamut of odd jobs around that theater department. "In fact," she said brightly, "your timing is perfect. Two things just came up. I got a call this morning from an old friend who's just started as artistic director at the Paramount on 42nd Street. They're all set to begin putting up a new *Hamlet*, only they don't have an assistant stage manager yet."

"Crewless at the Paramour?"

"Paramount. But that's not all. A friend of mine with the Princess Pessimissima collective just called. They're doing an experimental piece they're calling *Waiting for Godette* in a rehabbed boutique in Alphabet City, but their stage manager just quit. I gather she found God, but she found Him or Her in Oregon, so she's leaving town."

"Well, that's ironic," I said.

"What isn't? Anyway, neither of them has any time to play with, so I think you'd have a good shot. I'll give you their numbers if you want, but obviously, you can't do both."

"Which one do you think would be better?" I asked.

"Oh, I couldn't say," she managed to say. "You'll have to decide."

Assistant stage managing on Broadway, stage managing off it, two fantastic opportunities, either one could be my big break— BUT I COULDN'T DO BOTH. I HAD TO DECIDE. It was scarier than a horror movie. If I hadn't known her for four years already, and if I hadn't been the one to call, I would have sworn my old professor was a plant, sent to send me over the edge. Clearly, I would have to ride one of these *dei ex machinae* into the sunset. I just had to think. I thought, *I have to talk to G., I have to talk to B. I need to get their opinions.*

"Go for *Hamlet*, definitely," said B. "It's the greatest play of all time. 'To be or not to be....' No, there's no question. Hey, if I conjugate the verb 'to be' for you, would you hold it against me? When I get off work today?"

"Are you kidding?" asked G. "A chance to get in with Princess Pessimissima, those internationally renowned bad girls? Snap it up. Blow off the Bard. Without a doubt. Want to come over tonight?"

For once, I turned them both down. I thought I'd better sleep on this one, not *with* it, really sleep, perchance to dream up a preference. While sleeping on it, I dreamed we were all in bed together, me in the middle, G. on the right, B. on the left. The weird thing was, it was so tranquil, so restful, so happy, so sweet. I was pervaded with a sense of peace, such as I hadn't felt in almost two years. Then I wet the bed. Which woke me up, of course. Instantly, anxiety coursed back through me, and in that state of dampened disorientation I lay until the sun came up.

As it turned out, it was a classic case of you snooze, you lose. While I was sleeping too much like a baby, rehearsals were taking place in New York; empty spaces were filling themselves, the way they do in New York, instantly. New York is, in many ways, the furthest thing from nature, but they share this feature: they both abhor a vacuum. By the time I called the contacts my professor had given me, the posts in question had been filled for thirteen hours. I had missed my chances at professional and social advancement.

Embarrassed and broke, I went to see my parents once more. With my tail vacillating between my legs, I admitted that I would not be able to make my rent next month, and I asked them to lend me some money.

"So many young people these days," my mother said. "Trouble making ends meet. It's a tough world out there, isn't it?" My father saw it a little bit differently. "Young people these days. If they they're not riding high on the new technologies or trading stock like it's going out of style, they're moving back home," he said, as he wrote out a check. He held it up in the air before extending it to me, as though to stress how serious he was. "We're just giving you this money because moving back home is not on the menu. It's time to grow up." He gave me a big hug and a kiss.

As my mother waved from the door, she said, "Good luck. Let us know when you've made some changes, and we'll celebrate."

I deposited the check in the bank, and headed home. As I rounded the corner onto my street, I saw two people sitting on the stoop of my building. They looked familiar. They looked like they were nodding and laughing. For a moment there, I thought it might be my dream come true, but as I approached, I could see the sarcasm swelling in each gesture either one made. What a horrible coincidence, borne, I could see as I came within range, from what had originally been lovely gestures on both of their parts: a videotape beside him on the step, a beautiful loaf of whole-grain bread and a jar of jam resting next to her.

B. saw me first. "Here she comes," he said. "The center of the universe."

"You just hate feeling displaced, don't you?" G. said to him.

"I just hate sharing my lover with someone so righteous, and so wrong for her."

"You're a spoiled brat. You remind me of my baby brother in junior high, whines when he doesn't get what he wants," G. said to B.

"You remind me of someone I used to go out with," B. snapped back at G. I almost laughed, but then I realized he meant me. This couldn't be happening. It couldn't be that I was starting to cry, right there on the sidewalk. It wasn't funny anymore, or maybe it never had been funny. Or it was funnier than ever, but we were losing our senses of humor.

"Please..." I said, and stopped. But, please what? I couldn't say. Pure panic marched my feet up the stairs past them and into my building.

I went into my apartment and I sat down in my chair, the only easy thing in my life. I saw B. and G. staring at me, him grimacing from his photo on the endtable, her from her photo on the wall, squinting. They were making it hard for me to think. I got up and put the pictures in a drawer. I sat back down. Changes, my mother had recommended, but I doubted that she meant my decor. A thought suddenly hit me as though a rock had been thrown through the window. Tinkle of glass. Wrapped around the rock, a note that said, *You could get always get some temp work.* It probably would not be fulfilling, and it would by definition not be permanent, but it would bring in some cash, it would raise my flagging self-respect, and if I had to stifle my creativity by working a desk job for a while, there might at least be some compensatory cutie in the office. Perhaps most importantly, tomorrow would not be too late to call an agency. Of this I could be certain. Just like that—a new thought, a decision, a thimbleful of certainty. Maybe tomorrow it would also not be too late to begin to think clearly about my love life, figure out how to keep B. and/or G. hanging on, and/or not. There could be more decisions in the offing, each one leading to others. I decided I better slow down. At this rate, I feared, I might strip a gear. So I sat there and waited for the day's curtain to fall.

Two Alphabets

Authorize. Barbary. Carburize. Daedalus. Elegy. Fenderbend. Generate. Housearrest. Ironize. Jerryrig. Kilowatt. Licorice. Marrakesh. Numerate. Ordinal. Patronym. Quietus. Retrospect. Sonorous. Tenterhooks. Ululate. Vespertine. Westerner. Expletive. Yesterday. Zeroing.

A foreign language text

A is for alcohol, not accidentally.

Abdelhadi
Abrupt beginning, no?
Aïd el Kebir

All the light bulbs in the house burned out just now. Not all at once, but one by one, over the course of this excruciatingly long evening. It was almost a total coincidence.

Antidisestablishmentarianism. The hippies appropriated this historical handle for opposition to the withdrawal of state support (originally from the Church of England) to mean its opposite—to mean, keep the state off of our bodies, out of our minds, and out of Indochina—even while the next generation sitting at school desks elected to save it its pride of place as the longest word in the language, English. It held its own against the contemporary coinage of *supercalifragilisticexpialidocious* because the latter is, while longer, made up.

There appear to be only these possibilities:
> He, she. I. (More formally or generically) One. (Very occasionally) You. (Theoretically) We, they.

There appear to be only these possibilities:
> Eddie Frank Gus Hank
> Linda Mary Nick Norm
> Ray Rex Rick Roy Russ
> Shelley Susie Tom.

Awed is what I was, by the power of language (or was it sex?) to bring things into being. Over-awed perhaps, as I had yet to learn how frighteningly simple it is to invent people—two girls and a guy standing on the roadside, shook up, the worse for wear, the varsity jackets that betray them as foreigners hanging open, red haze, pretty faces, her lips, his clean-shaven chin, the other one's green eyes—for the purpose of their destruction. You would wish to be acquainted with these young and pretty people, to have them travel unharmed a while longer. I would too; there is nothing I want more. They don't even appear to know enough to be scared, as at the side of the road they wait to understand the consequences of what just happened. Red haze. Each of the three avoids looking at the other two. The guy walks around to the other side of the car.

There was a car crash. A driver lost control. Those words bear with them an image and the automatic question of people involved. Are they our young friends? Bent, burned, and smoking. Shattered. The echo of a squeal to a halt. That's the automobile, probably. But had there been a fourth figure—wouldn't you expect so—another guy? Now you have a bad accident in mind. Yours could not possibly be the same as mine, but each one dramatizes the sudden and radical disfigurement of our most everyday expectations. Neither of our imagined crash scenes could render accurately the postures of the three, their expressions, what they know or don't know, but there they are.

Drizzle hovers over the new landscape. The accident sizzles into the coal gray evening.

Because there are 26 letters in the English alphabet, the possibilities of the English language do not exceed the following—or do they:

26 one-letter words plus 26-squared two-letter words, plus 26-cubed three-letter words, plus 26-to-the-fourth four-letter

words, plus 26-to-the-fifth five-letter words. Etc. Up to the 28th power. See above.

Bicycle, blue, on which my neighbor, Abdelhadi, accidentally rode through the scene and saw the car that had been parked up the hill all week, surrounded by three small fires and two dazed young women, but when he stopped to try talking to these last two, he found that they spoke only English. Wait, he tried to tell them, wait here. He thinks maybe he saw another figure on the other side of the car, echo of a familiar jacket, as he jumped back on his bike and flew for bi- or trilingual help. A minute later, he heard a big boom, he says. But he was already around two bends, couldn't see back, and kept rolling forward, figuring that he should just keep going, not lose any time. Blue bicycle with empty baskets going home.

when in the iron cage
seize the cage bars
    bend them bend them

the spongiform bars of the cage
    bend them

It was not in order to create a carbon copy of myself that I had a kid. I had a kid because that was what one did in the old days; one married the prettiest girl at college who wasn't already engaged to someone else, and one had a kid. Before that, one, or two, really, had sex, of course. In those days.

Carcass, or should I say corpse

In this case, local color is not a device. It happens to designate my neighbors, my friends. Foreigners trekking around Morocco typically notice the black and blond deserts, the red mountains, the green oases snaking alongside the few riverbeds, and in spring, the pink blossoms of the almond trees, under the famously azure sky. The famously sheltering azure sky. These features of the landscape are *unique au monde*. But if those travelers see Abdelhadi and his compatriots at all, they see someone exotic, strange, and even greedy and/or stupid, judging by the way they avert their eyes from the racks of pottery and geodes by the roadside, and haltingly address him and the other men who sit at the outdoor tables at the village café. He is anything but. He is perceptive, inventive, and as kind as the day is long to his wife and children, to his parents, and to his friends, who, he says, include me. I am the strange one, whom he and Hicham and Jallah and Karim condescend to address in French because my Arabic remains rudimentary.

Common: there is nobody that something like this hasn't happened to; there is nobody that exactly this *has* happened to.
Compound prepositions, among others: according to, apart from, as to, aside from, because of, instead of, on account of, out of, up in.

Conjunctions
Dark house

Defamiliarization

The dream is always the same. The dream is always the same, always different versions of infinitely expanding architecture, lots of apartment hunting with the historic wings unfolding as my ex-wife and I take the guided tour through and among the treasures; visiting other people's precocious houses poised farther and farther over the water, or merging magically with the forest or the hill—nooks and crannies and hidden staircases forever; institutional numbers with all the trappings—the doors and corridors and correctional officers, and the labyrinth of functional buildings. Random House.

Eight years old. That's the age he was when I left. Eight, nine, ten, etc. Up to 23. See below.

Either, neither.

Evening. Meaning *what?*—so many things, not nearly enough. Less and more than night.
Faith, or lack thereof.

Fête du Sacrifice
Flesh of my flesh, out of my flesh, because of my flesh, finally apart from, forever apart from, my flesh.

Funny. *What* is so funny.

Sniffing gasoline…. Why do so many people get high? So many different ways?

You'll think I was, but I wasn't exactly, a hippie; I was both too young and too old. Or too straight and too smart. I did marry. I did work a job. But I guess it must have been a fairly strong counter-cultural impulse that drove me out of my old life in the States. The will to cliché got me coming and going.

His name is not Roy or Ray or Ed or Hank or Tom. Or Nick. His girlfriend's name is not Linda or Shelley. That's obvious, right?

Houses, and more houses. Mud-walled and built by hand. Cool to the touch.

Huts with thatched roofs. About fifteen years ago now, I left the big city, the big country; I left the apartment blocks and the grid-iron and moved abroad. I went native, as they say. Fifteen years later, I was hosting a small gathering in the particular house I call my own, with four young people, not seven kilometers from where they crashed and not half an hour before. Before of. Before from. One of them is mine. It couldn't be worse. Is it too late for *before* again, or at least *instead?*

I don't have a car. My rusty bike, so long unused it seems ready to grow roots, is a laughing matter in the village. I am to wait here, Abdelhadi says. I trust him.

I have a very close relationship with language. It and I are intimate.

Inconceivable: I may never see the face of my child again.
Indelible, inedible, in-fucking-credible

Interior monologue
Interjections
In the belly of the beast, and then again, out of it

when in the iron cage
seize the cage bars
    bend them bend them

It is not from Italian, the language of love, but from mathematics, the language of physics, that we draw our rule. Numbers, permutations, factorials. Glory be to mathematics which reminds us of certain truths: dismal, inescapable, with bars. I moved away but I have not managed to lose my math.

I've read a lot of shit by people like me back home. If there are any other possibilities, I need to know now, not later. NOW.

Just when I thought I could breathe easy. He had become an adult, *like* an adult, and he drove himself here from the airport on the other side of the mountains in a rented car, and his girlfriend with him. I was so pleased that he wanted me to meet this grenadine-eyed girl. She was warm, and she got in several good puns, and although they stayed for days, she didn't wear one outfit that didn't leave her belly winking out from between her shirt and her shorts. I mean, she was cute. And they seemed happy. In the final hours, another young couple, friends from school who'd been backpacking around the area, came over for drinks, after which they all took off together. Literally into the sunset. Or rather onto it, as they trudged up the hill toward the road where anyone with a car has to leave it parked because the only way into my place is to walk. The last time I saw him, he was superimposed on the setting sun.

Kidding myself
King Mohammad VI. Like his father before him, King Hassan II, he holds the post for which there are no nominees.

Lessons in a foreign language

Red Light Green Light:
    Make meaning
    Make meaning
    Make meaning
    Stop making sense

Lift off
Left off
Left of center

Mansions: maybe somebody's father's house has many, but not me, not mine, not in my house, goddamn it.

Maybe something like this has happened to you.

The meter is the basic measure of distance, the unit from which all other measures of distance, whether longer or shorter, are derived: centimeter and millimeter no less than kilometer. Here in the metric system.

Midriff

Mother tongue

My biggest mistake: not to say to him: Don't let him drive, the other guy. I didn't say it because I thought it was obvious the guy was drunk, and obvious that someone who couldn't meet my hand to shake it without concentrating on the gesture should not drive. At least one of these things may not have been obvious to the four young adults who left my hut after a pleasant cocktail hour of sorts just before the mosquitoes kicked in. I clasped my own little guy in a big square hug, and he let me, for the first time in years, which confirmed what I suspected as he came down the hill at the beginning of the visit: he was finally taller than me.

My hut is a very very very nice hut. I must have brought with me a brain full of songs I'd heard on the radio.

Next and last... forever
Next to last

Ninety percent of conversations in English are composed of the same 200 words, sociolinguists have proven, by way of mathematics. Math persuades me. And it's easy to imagine which 200 words they are: the substanceless kind we can't live without, the dust mites and pillars of our speech: pronouns, and conjunctions, and half the prepositions. The article. Imagine a part of speech so important to the ecology of English that even though it has only three members, it deserves a category unto itself. Such are the articles. And how do they function? They introduce the nomials, the nominals—no no, that's not right—the noun or nouns. The difference between *the* and *a* is the difference between one and many. There is no article for none, for zero, for used to exist, but there should be.

Obviously, his name is not Nick.

Offal. This is the most awful night I could ever imagine, the worst delivery of news, impossible now and tomorrow, too, to swallow. Don't let Abdelhadi come again, bringing any more of that shit around here.

On dreams in narrative prose, consider:
  – type of language
  – length
  – placement (when)
  – how many characters do it
  – function

On viscera and evisceration, consider the following and the forego-ing.

The order of things: younger becomes older, shit is passed down, flows downhill, floats downstream, older dies before younger. Ring out the old, ring in the new. From up to down is the order of things. It doesn't matter that this is untrue, or rather that it is arbitrary. It doesn't matter that you could argue that down to up is the order of things, or that what goes down must come up, or that what comes around goes around, or is it vice versa? You'd be right. So what. Many orders work; this happens to be my elected one. If I must add this order to my list of wrong choices, I will never understand anything again. I will cry until morning which will be night.

The ordinary, the occasional, the extraordinary. Imitation of the one real, negation of the idea of a one-and-only real, any realistic unreal. These seem to be the possibilities.

Or so you'd think. And so I've thought, lo these many years of words and dissatisfaction.
out from under inside between see above metal reworked in any new inferno please

How to Outwit Yourself
Parsing sentences

Personal pronouns, also of which there are very few, soldiers in the war between the sexes, the agonizing rucksack of history on their camouflaged backs. Prepositions, of which there are more than articles to with from, form another part of speech. Proper nouns: Kiddo, Buddy, Pal.

Pomegranate-wine drunkard
Possessives. My son, not yours, not *yours*, and not *his* either to drive off the side of the goddamned road.

These seem to be the possibilities:
    I You He She. One. We You They.
These seem to be the possibilities:
    Ray, Roy, Norm. Nick.

These seem to be the possibilities.

The potholes, the goddamned potholes. But no, it couldn't have been the potholes. The potholes would blow out a tire, unalign an axle at worst. They wouldn't send a car off the side of the road.

Prison through *prism*

Perhaps I should qualify. You get a few infinite categories, after all: nouns, verbs, and their qualifications. There—oh joy—is the range, the expressivity associated with language, and the invention and naming of the new.

How different the sense if I had written: There was a *cat* crash. It would not have been quite so serious.

Radio range, getting out of it

Rainbow, which broke out like an irony. There had been no rain beforehand. I know that spot of road and I can imagine the rainbow over their heads as they crawled out of, up from, onto the embankment, if you could call it an embankment. Red light green light blue light for a moment suspended over my head, barely visible in the evening sky that would in another moment swallow even the indigo, and I smiled at the joke at the time, because Abdelhadi had not yet reached the village on his bike.

The end of Ramadan is marked with a sheep-sacrificing festival—*Aïd el Kebir, Fête du Sacrifice*—that commemorates what Abraham did not have to do to Isaac. In the story, the deed was ultimately displaced onto a member of a lower order caught in the brambles nearby. On the first day of the festival, which falls next week this year, Moroccans ritually slaughter sheep and cook and eat only the hearts and brains. On the second day, they move on to other parts, the intestines; on the third, they smoke the meat. Shofar sho good—until this year.

Reading, writing, and arithmetic. I brought these with me, along with a duffel bag of clothes, which have faded and frayed.

Really, the festival is a party. No harm done. On the contrary, everyone is happy cooking and feeding themselves and their families and friends. One year, this party fell during spring break and the kid came over and we brought home a length of the intestines that Abdelhadi's wife, Leila, had given us, and laid it out like the tracks of a train set. You could say we played with our food, but, or because, we were unaccustomed to the taste. You could say I'm no bloody Abraham.

Rebel

Reference works, of which I brought two: a dictionary and *Words Into Type*, the latter being the kind of book you used to see on the shelves of editors and copy-editors, with everything you could ever want to know about grammar, preparation of manuscripts, typography, and illustrations. And proofing. And use of words. Almost. Everything you need to bring Shit Into Being. The kind I used to see. And need. After a couple of years here, I could not look at this book anymore without its acronym jumping out at me: *WIT*. But I could not see the humor. *WIT* makes an excellent doorstop, for propping open the door on the many blue days when the only visitor will be a butterfly. If that. I might as well throw the dictionary on top of it now.

Reject
Round-house

Same numerical situation in French, for example, only the particular 200 words are different. For instance, instead of *glue-sniffing*, the French use the word *wine-drinking*.

Shit. Shit shit shit. Oh shit. *Oh shit*, they said, those guys in that movie, as they jumped, and the scenery mounted behind them as they plunged down. I haven't been to a movie in fifteen years, but I used to see one every week. I think I took that *shit* too seriously. I didn't realize how young they were, those guys.

Sometimes life's not easy; other times, it's hard.
Spill ink. As with oil, blood, and, famously, milk, it's no use crying.

Sometimes it's charred.

Tense doesn't begin to describe it; nor tenses them.

Tents

That's the difference between conversation and literature, my friends—74,000 minus 200 odd words *and...*

The guy was out of it, my son's friend. It was obvious to me.

These are the possibilities.

The tide comes up and goes out in the toilet.... That is the order of things. Do I really have running water and electricity in my mud house? Yes, and that's just one of the hypocrisies I still practice.

To be, to do, to get, to have, to want. Some say those are all the verbs you need. With verbs, you always get four for the price of one, because each one has these possible constructions: affirmative, negative, interrogative, negative interrogative. I say, not *to go? to need, to write?* Not *to need to go write?*

La transcription de l'arabe dans l'alphabet latin n'obéit pas à des règles rigoureuses.

Travel

Trip

Under certain conditions, the dream of a house can hurt like real life.

...and a couple of advanced degrees. Which I had under my belt, and used to append to my name in initials before I realized I could do my work anywhere. It was theoretically possible.

You-niversal

Unreliable utilities. That's what we have here. So when I read, late into the night, and the light suddenly goes out, I don't know if it's the bulb or the electricity. I always assume it's the electricity. I'm not always right.

Varsity athletics explains my son's friend's jacket. The dude said he was on the soccer team, when I asked. He pointed to the little soccer ball on the sleeve. Although he was just a fan, my son has had has an almost identical jacket, except for the soccer ball, like the girls'. Two guys in similar jackets, one of whom may still be standing in or near a ditch by the side of the road. It is a possibility.

Prepositions that are an inseparable part of a verb should be capped:
> Getting Down to Cases;
> How to Lay Off a Line Through a Given Point That Shall Be Parallel to a Given Line;
> Things to Do With and Find Out About a Book... A Pomegranate. A Rental Car.
>> A Parental Figure. A Soccer Ball. A Wool Blanket. Electricity. The History of a People. The Iron Cage. A Ticket Stub. A Handprint. Mud. But I regress.

One way out of your wits is to have a child.

We'll see.
How will I—what we used to call—cope? How?
What

What can I say? If I have outlived my child, I will never understand anything again. If I left him when he was young, it was not because I did not need to be in the presence of his growing body. It was not because I was not fascinated by the rate of expansion of his vocabulary. It was not because his handprint in clay was not the most precious piece of art I owned. It was not because his cocked head and his questions were only casually beautiful. They were not. His curiosity was acutely, hugely, bone-warmingly sweet. And it was not because I could tolerate his cries. I could not. Nevertheless.

What's *next*? Or rather, *where's* next? Because it's absent from the list of prepositions in the book. And what about *next to*? Isn't that a compound preposition? What am I missing?

When I left, he was eight years old. It was because I could not tolerate his mother, my mother, the city, the hypocrisy in which the higher professions are saturated. When I thought that the stub of an airplane ticket was proof that I had in fact left, I was still naïve. When I left, he asked me, "Daddy, can I come to your new house with you?" even though he had stopped calling me "Daddy" the year before. And he *had* come to my new house, several times over the years. When I thought that his visits, filled with arguments but also camping and lessons in packing and laying a mud brick with hair and straw knit up in it, and, more recently, Scrabble, which he brought two trips ago—when I thought that those visits were proof that you can never lose a child even if you abandon him, I was as yet totally untutored in loss.

When? In the iron cage.

Wool blankets brown and white like sheep. These we stretched and hung from sticks we stuck in the sand at the corners of our camp, brown and concave shelter sagging between us and the aforementioned sky. They colored our differing dreams different darks while we slept.

Why did I not encourage or even coerce him into learning the local language? I felt I didn't have the right. He went and studied classics, dead languages, more irony than I can take.

96

Words for this? *You* tell *me.*

Words Into Type, page 381: about, above, across, after, against, along, amid, among, around, at, athwart, before, behind, below, beneath, beside, between, beyond, by, concerning, during, except, excepting, for, from, in, inside, into, of, off, on, onto, out, outside, over, past, pending, regarding, respecting, round, since, through, throughout, till, to, toward, under, underneath, until, unto, up, upon, with, within, without.

Examples precede and follow.
Expatriate. Ugly word.

Exterior monologue

Youth

You. Yes you.

Zzz. Into and out of the dark night, at around and ever after midnight, on and off the lights. Who shuts his eyes sees houses going on and on and on.

Kant Get Enough

A long time ago, I cut my teeth on poets. That was then. I fuck philosophers now, even though they talk too much. With delectable precision, philosophers delight themselves no end tying you up in traffic. Circles, jams, and lights. The endless propositions. The turtle-necked casuistry. But when they come to the panties, they go wild. That's when you hear them huffing and puffing Schopenhauer. I get down on the floor and shake it with the last school of thought that bumped and ground its way into this poor schlub's philosophizing heart. I don't care if it's yesterday I'm spreading them for.

I don't care either what their stuff is made of. As long as their logic is airtight, I consider any stiff wunderkind, any old bratwurst, any baguette worthy of a romp. Arendt you glad I didn't say "banana?" As long as they save the unknowability routine for the timeless questions, I'll fuck philosophers time and time again. Is it any coincidence we do it Western style, my Nietzsche's up over my head, panties pushed to the side like everything south or east of Greece? Philosophers—they can't think their way out of a rib cage but oh the infinite splitting of the hairs, the ever-nerveless hairs. Hey girl, let's go down to the annual convention: Hobbes, knobs, and Engels. Quad Erotic Demonstratum. If you don't like the fragments or should I say the fragmentary nature of my discourse, you can kiss my Aristotle. Which looks and feels and tastes so good. We won't let a little thing like a podium get in our way—or will we?

I prefer philosophers at breakfast, better yet before dawn—less conversation, at least until the coffee kicks in. The light of Descartes is dangerous and seems to open the way for bursts of unsolicited commentary. A risk worth taking on the whole, but on the other hand, fuck philosophers, with their right way to do this and that. Around evening time, they try to get colloquial with me. *Pull up to my bumper, baby*, kidding around, quotation marks. Fuck philosophers. With their assessment of the way I turn a phrase. *Assess this*, I say, and I roll the tip of my tongue across my perfect teeth.

Fuck fucking *philosophy*, an occupation I used to find unusual in a man. Until I was nineteen. Not to mention a woman. More baloney logicians out there than you could shake a stick at. But why would you? That's the kind of joke you're likely to hear from the analytic types. A little shop talk never hurt, but sense of humor can be a problem. When it is, I say, *Take it to the movie theater, Wittgenstein, blow it in and out your own ear on the head of a pin in the dark.* Just another Freud Day afternoon matinee, matey.

What we got here, this here's a party, a big savage party for me and my philosopher friends. It's the most fun when I can get them to let their Kierkegaard down. One swings by another's house in a horn-rimmed automobile to pick him up and bring him to the party, about half past eight, hazards flashing, singing, "Now dearie, don't be Plato." They wanna be there when the glands start playing.

"Knock Knock!!"

"Who's there?" Or would it be Hume in this case?

Enter nineteen philosophers. I greet them in a little black number with a see-through tautology. Cerebrate, cerebrate; dance to the music. It's a little awkward at first, but I give them high Marx for trying. Why it gets good, though, this party's rhetorical.

Rhetorical the way a philosopher, once stony now stoned, commands me to take off my shirt. Now I tug at one sleeve, now tug at the other, freeing my shoulders, my tits, and my ribs, binding my arms to my sides with the neck of my shirt stretched kinky at my elbows. Rhetorical the hooting and Husserl in a circle of which I am the putative center. Rhetorical the *Shake them, baby, shake them.* I say, *Now we're talking*. Rhetorical the *Give us some pussy*. I say, *Make me*. I don't mean it, I'm just heightening the suspense. I dance, half naked: hemline, free will, and nipples. Boldly the first one, shyly, the next few, the philosophers whip out their Schlegels; now *they're* heightening the suspense. Working my hands around to the front, I suddenly flap my skirt. Up. Yup, the panties do it again. Pandemonium. Rhetorically we go to bed, since the literal bed is too small for all of us and the floor will do as well. Guess what we're batting around now, not just good ideas.

Yes, they drive me crazy, but when it's an argument I'm looking for, philosophers deliver. When I want to hear it broken down, why I should give it up. When I want to be begged, pleaded with, or otherwise cajoled. I like the fucking better when the foreplay is well-reasoned. I get off on hearing about the degrees of torture, akin to Aquinas of thirst, that this highly particular philosopher would suffer if he or she could not get into my pants. Oh the miscarriage of justice, they complain, when I send a lousy *carpe diem* packing. You can put a better Spinoza on it than that, I say. For I am a connoisseur of seduction lines and textual proclivities. I've collected them for ages: philosophers and their come-ons and pretexts (and whatever comes next), but they have to be good. Philosophers're not ideal, they talk too much, but at least they talk enough.

The last three years, a thousand nights of persuasion, while I worked up to nineteen of them. The thousand nights of passionate pleading. The new meaning of "make believe," which would have exhausted Scheherazade. The thousand nights of making my lovers make me believe they want to sleep with me, they need to sleep with me, and my favorite: it'll be the best thing that ever happened to me. Ergo. Apparently infinite variations thereon. If you can make me believe it, I'll open up the curly gates and we'll have a Heidegger time.

Next morning, after a quick breakfast, out they go. *Bundle up,* I say, *you'll catch your death of God.* And come back now, you hear, when you're ready to rev it up again with a brand new, flawless, paradigm-shattering proof that I have a hot ass and you absolutely have to have it too. In the meantime, I go upstairs and I rinse out my panties.

Why I'm Jealous

Why I'm jealous of Mary Jo LoBello Jerome:

Because she has a long O sound in each of her three names (if you count Mary Jo as one, which she says she does) and two such sounds in one of them, LoBello. And in addition to assonance, consonance. She's rolling in it. With two L sounds nested between two J sounds, themselves framed by two R sounds, which are in turn tucked in between the motorboat hum of M's, she's a walking, talking palindrome. Oh to sound so beautiful as Mary Jo LoBello Jerome and to own the most sonorous name. Mmmm. Lucky Mary Jo.

Why I was jealous of Jody Condotta:

Because she got all Excellents on her report card, while I got all Excellents—except for one Very Good. My Very Good was in Penmanship, and indeed, Jody's Penmanship was better than mine. On this there could be no two opinions: my print was herky-jerky, my cursive merely legible. But my Spelling was Excellent. I watched Jody change her answer from *embarass* to *embarrass* after looking at my test. Her Penmanship was Excellent enough that she could emend her answers on spelling tests and still hand in tests that looked like passports freshly stamped by God. *Freind* to *friend*. Of course, as a good child citizen, I would never have told on Jody—unless there had been a category for Ethical Conduct. Then we would both have had all Excellents except for one Very Good. Righteous injury resulting from true injustice does not soothe the sores of jealousy. It's just another sore. Oh for a simple balm for my cheating heart.

Why I'm jealous of Alyssa Longo:

Because she lives with the man I love. Because she gets to call him Car, Carito, Carlos, Honey, hers, while I can only call him Carlos. Carlos. I call him it on the phone, and yes, indeed, he'll meet with me and go over the next scene, which he does with his feet flat on the floor, fully shod, in complete compliance with the obsolete Hays Code. The only nude in the room is bronze and inert. We work at his oak table, in the tranquil home he and Alyssa share; we collaborate, while the hypotenuse of afternoon arcs down to meet the base, Carlos roundly untroubled by my presence. Carlos is crazy about my script; he's invested in it, will realize it, believes we may have a hit on our hands. Carlos even likes my memos. But I guess he doesn't like them enough. Carlos's Memorandum of Understanding is all for Alyssa. His certainty, my uncertainty, and our edits for the better unspool on the table; we work so well together; how oh how can he not want to touch too? Oh Carlos, I would trouble you. Enter Alyssa, Carlos's fingers on the page, *here,* and *here* (to measure time elapsed), and there they stay when he looks up to say hi, square with her, not a shadow of a shadow on his face. Off the page come those fingers, as she approaches, around her waist they wind. Then letting go of her, Carlos's hands act the parts for Alyssa, show her the blocking, vibration indicating speech. Once, Carlos admired my professionalism, which goes to show that Carlos doesn't know me as well as I know him. What I admire is Carlos's flat fingernails, the topaz thumbpad that presses

Alyssa's lips before he kisses her. Carlos's fingers enter Alyssa. Vibration indicating sound of "Carlos Carlos *now*." On that same oak table, perhaps—no, not when I am there. Alyssa, absolutely unafraid of mild me, leaves us alone again in the dimming room. In about a half-hour, the three of us will go out for dinner and her jealous-bonelessness will get me in the ticker, which to fortify I will drink a little too much rosé. Oh Carlos, leave the lovely Alyssa and the silly pink wine—let's break away, baby, I'll show you the meaning of *co-produce*, we could ticket to the moon, lover, I'm calling you the one I want and cannot ever have.

Why I was jealous of Regina Jones:

Because when we played gypsy princess, pretend night fell every hour or so, to break up the monotony of hot flamenco days—or for the sake of realism because real time features its own punctuating darkness—and each time it did, I was weary, exhausted in fact, and I wanted to rest. When I lay down on those gypsy princess nights in Regina's apartment, I wasn't faking. Regina would crouch down for ten seconds and then she would bounce up and scream, "It's morning," choking on her cape in her great hurry to simulate another day. I would grumble, as though I might not yet have been woken by her kicking me in the side. "No, it's not morning yet," I would say, as though I needed a shave and a cup of joe, and me only in third grade at the time, but Regina ruled the gypsy princess cosmos, so it was morning every hour. I was jealous of Regina because nine years of living hadn't yet worn her out, as I believed they had done me. Oh for a red cape. For the strength to smash the day like cymbals.

Why I'm jealous of Bruno Badour:

Because he thinks he's such a bloody good writer. I'm sure Bruno is a fucking genius and I'm sure I'm not even fit to suck his cock, but can't I? Can't I anyway suck his cock? Even though I don't deserve to? Can't I be Bruno and suck it myself? Can't I just once take for granted, like the fixity of the distance between my face and the floor, the idea that my spume is very special, very valuable stuff, even if I don't have his prize-winning cock loafing between my legs? Oh to find that fiction of self credible. For eight or ten solid hours. For that experience, I would gladly pay $25,000, to be submitted in bureaucracy-sized installments to the Bursar of the Underwhelmed. For that, I would rub raw my application, my need, my simpering plea, my craven confession—I admit, I don't have what it takes, guys—my gimme begging, here on bended knee, and my knees of course are already raw. Just from sucking Bruno's cock in my mind. That's how potent that motherfucker is. Déjà raw. For just a brief flash of self-sucking thoroughgoing love of me, myself, I would remit my stub. I would tender my tender, my ass, my legal tender. I would put this chick in the mail, however crude it sounds, dirtier than riding naked on a mudflap. For Bruno's cow-faced ease of mind, for Bruno's brutality, for Bruno's conviction that he is more than good, he is better than most, easily including me and all the others, for Bruno's caucasian idiot eyes and his neutral hair—listen, he doesn't care, his hair doesn't have to be great. My hair has to be great. I'm jealous because Bruno's mediocre hair is more than made up for by his stunning prose. My hair meanwhile has to be great because it's all I've got going on between my knees and the ceiling. Oh to walk in Bruno's shoes for a day.

Why I was jealous of Jody Condotta all over again:

Because she showed me up once more, years later. When Jody and her pet parrot got kidnapped by her pedestrian parents, who opted for the safety and complacence of Passaic over the risk and stimulation of the city, Jody skipped a grade, as any little sophisticate repotted in suburban soil might do. A mutual friend, left behind like me, conveyed this acid intelligence. For Manhattan me, Passaic, like everything across any river, didn't even make the map, so although her promotion in the hinterlands rankled me, I was sure she had bested me, however backhandedly, for the last time. Because who comes back from Pluto, after all? Old Jody does. Eight years later, I landed as a freshman at the college she had come, unbeknownst to me, to own the year before. And when I did, trunk barely plunked on the smooth wood floors of Oratory Hall, she acted the gracious sophomore, calling to welcome me, to invite me to dinner, to show me the ropes. Or was it to lord her Excellent Vocabulary over me? "Why don't you meet me at six at the sarcophagus?" she asked. Why not just hand me the rope and skip dinner? What I said, blasé as I could, was "Oh, I don't know," but what I didn't know was what a *sarcophagus* is. Oh, sure, I do now; I found it out.

Why I'm jealous of Leonora Parra:

Because she has a dark-haired baby girl. Because she lives in the most beautiful nineteenth-century yellow clapboard farmhouse on the edge of a field, pumpkin patch, bird sanctuary, occasional grazing of sheep, home to brambles and berries. Home, also, to a perfect dark-haired baby girl. The baby is only six months old and already Leonora is back in her study surrounded by lovely small furniture she found on the street, which makes her home homier than real antiques would. Her glance restores former junk to vital poignancy, the fragments of enamel and glass, no matter how prosaic, radiate belonging, true blue on their irregular shelves, there in her raftered study with the smell of mold beaten back to the mild aroma of a grandma. The study and the two rooms beside it house a collection of rare books and manuscripts from the seventeenth century, the finest in the state, which Leonora has cultivated and traded for and preserved with cutting-edge techniques camouflaged by the casual. There she is, Leonora, sitting in the resonant mote-swirling study where her plans for expansion blossom in the warbled light of the sun as it subsides through the age-old windows and curls into a braid on the free-from-the-garbage rug. Oh my sunlight should curl in braids in the dry heat. I should have hot dry expensive books. I should have a dark-haired baby girl. The baby's flat pig face, beyond cute, her black eyelashes arching away from her swimmy gray eyes like an architectural feat, her pudgy clammy hands toying with the air, with the idea of standing up, maybe, someday. Even beyond the library, the baby's home is exquisite, in a not-too-precious kind of way. There's a down-to-earth, country-bohemian, cleaned-weekly, never-scrubbed kind of style there, which can be found on page 372 of the catalogue, but why buy the stuff when you can find it waiting for you free on the street the night before it's crushed and hauled away. For me, it's the catalogue or nothing. Oh the delivery should be express. May it arrive tomorrow.

Why I'm jealous of my older sister:

Because there's always going to be one smart-ass in the crowd who thinks, "That's not *why* you're jealous. That's *how* you're jealous." And only an older sibling has the license to say it out loud, the right not to pad it with civility, but to issue it with a mocking tone that overlooks the fact that jealousy is a picador who's bleeding me. And if that sibling has shown paintings in the Biennale, what has that got to do with it. All she sees is red and me as bull, and all she says is, "Those are not reasons, those are descriptions." That's right, Einstein, I'm jealous because it's the only response I can think of to people who have something I want that I don't have, or have something I want that I do have, or have something I don't want that makes them happier than the things that I want that I do have make me. I can't help it. Why I'm jealous, therefore, is that I'm unreasonable, by reason of unrequited vanity. I'm small and bitter, almost asphyxiated by my very mediocrity, but not quite. Are you happy now? Leonora says anger doesn't make for good literature, but I say, "*Bullshit.*" I can only hope it's so. Opining that Bruno knows better, Leonora points to the stack of rejections I wish I had the *huevos* to recycle. I point to Carlos, who has moved on to the next project. Oh woe is *sole mio.*

Why I'm jealous of Mary Jo LoBello Jerome all over again:
Because her middle name is Rose, she tells me now, after all this time. And if a rose is a rose is a rose, and on like that it logically goes, when will it ever end? Stop this train, I want to get off.

Why I'm jealous of Chaim Lowe:
Because Chaim vacations in a psych ward when the going gets tough. It's not the rotten glamour of *Will There Really Be a Morning?* or the sentimental cruelty in *One Flew Over the Cuckoo's Nest* that attracts me. And I'm only a little bit jealous of shots of Thorazine. What I envy, in the main, is the letting it go, the letting it slide,

the needing to be done for and the being done. Because the going does get tough. I'm not crazy, though, so I perform a quotidian calculus, asking myself how long people I know would take care of me before they tired of wiping the food off my face and turned me over to professional wipers, strangers on staff. I do a cost-benefit analysis of playing a matador—of going round and round in that revolving door—nothing like the analysis of a real madhatter. Chaim here, he strains credibility a little bit further every time he takes another handful of pills, but what really drives us batty is that when we come to wipe, which we do in shifts for as long as he's in, he flashes the sweet grin he just couldn't muster when he was out. If it were me in the bin, me in the bin, me in the bin behind the grin, I might be crazy enough not to care who wiped me, which would be my only luck, because you just know there would be some unattended shifts. As it is, I'm not crazy, so I realize that this particular envy is in bad taste, insensitive even. And also because I'm not crazy, my insensitivity is A for Average, not special, of course. O for Ordinary, according to my therapist. I come to no good end, but I come to no bad one either—no madness or death, no love or success—leaving only the coda, tacked on to an endlessly endless refrain. Oh to drool like a loveable nut, an extraordinary fool, to babble like an idiot or sweat like a star, to discover the cure for the middle of the road, to flatten out the bell curve with pioneering math, to endow an award for the mean, to break the ribbon or the mold, to be the first or last, the best or worst, the most or least, to be especially anything or superlatively nothing. Not to be so so-so, no.

Who Writes This Shit?!

You're in your first year of college in the North, where you've always lived, and the boy you're in love with tells a room full of people that the music to which he would commit suicide is Pachelbel's Canon. He would do it in a bathtub. The two of you are sitting around a smoky dorm room with your thirteen closest friends, playing the old parlor game that takes for granted that all fifteen of you would kill yourselves. Winter leaks in through the double-hung windows. The poppers offer everyone a microcosmic inhalant death, a temporary taste of it, mildly illegal, as they make their liquid way around the room. The first week of the fall semester, you fell in love with this boy in your U.S. History course over the last cigarette in your pack, which you shared at his request during the break, and underneath whose smoke the boy informed you that where he is from the Civil War is still being fought, the gray uniforms still being spun in the factories, the embers still shifting, and his father and his father's mother and his grandmother's father are tired, but none of them is more tired than he, the boy, from trying to get the South back up on its feet again, black and white together. In the bathtub in your mind, one vein or another would open to the swelling strings and he would close his eyes to the lukewarm tune of generations gone. The boy you're in love with is eerily convincing, and the Canon promises more perfect accompaniment than any of the other music mentioned by your peers.

That summer, when you are visiting the boy in a state you have never seen except frosted onto a glass from a gas station in the blue North (in the days when they gave out free presents with the petroleum your father paid for), the two of you share a chocolate milkshake in a coffee joint, like a flashback to the time when this southern state was freshly frosted onto that gas-station glass. The Jim Crow in the milkshake unnumbs your tongues. Neither of you is so old or so wise as you suspect. Coming down off the coke, you begin to say that you never realized that *Mary Poppins* was so political until you saw it just now, when the Muzak strains of Pachelbel's Canon start piping into the coffee shop. The two of you raise four eyebrows, and one of you says, *Who writes this shit?*

The boy you're in love with no longer loves you that way, if he ever did—and now that you think back, you remember that either you or he usually passed out before making love on any given occasion, or was it always and every given occasion, although you thought of yourselves as lovers—and now he never could, ever since the moment, earlier in the summer, when he saw one of the guys with whom he was organizing a counter-rally to a Klan march dancing at the only men's club in town with an interracial clientele. It was the guy whose presence made him feel so strangely warm that time they sat, leaflets on their knees, in silence in the pick-up truck, in the cool dawn before the morning headed south, first steaming up the windows of the truck, then dancing there before him in the club. He saw him dancing there. Then, then, then, the boulders of history sprung up weightless and twirled and flashed on the dance floor like glittering confetti, intoxicating. The boy claims he didn't know what kind of club it was until he got there. He apologizes. You are still in love with this boy, just as you were a minute ago, so ash or no ash in your mouth, you blow a mocha bubble to his future, and you mean it. Let him not replace Pachelbel with disco in the doom scenario of the age; let him, still dancing, stamp out fires for years to come. Perhaps this latest turn

112

of events explains his sudden taste for Julie Andrews. You feel what you never felt at school: the freedom to shuck off the suicide routine; unsure; the opposite of tired. Can you come to the club with him and his new boyfriend, do they have any girls there?

That night, you go to the club which for all its mystery holds nothing you didn't imagine, except for the girl at the end of the bar who asks with her eyebrows what kind of drink you like, and you snort: laughter, white and black fairy dust, that fast you are in love with someone new. Now, as one song seems ready to segue into the next, the girl with the arched face moves toward you, looking about ready to reach through the confetti and ask you to dance, until she suddenly halts on account of the new song which, swear to god, is a hip-hop cover of Pachelbel's Canon. Before her face can go from question to quiz—from, Can we dance? to Can we dance to *this?*—you spin around toward the boy you used to be in love with, who has seen and heard it all and, grinning, punches you lightly in the arm—recognition!—and together the two of you scream, *Who writes this shit?!* which is lost in the music, and in the laughter of the girl who knows nothing other than her next move, which is to order you a White Russian. It's her best guess and it's not bad.

How not bad you'll tell her tomorrow as you two watch the sun slide up out of the newspaper in the morning, and you'll tell her how not bad again, whispering into the nap on her neck as you and she make like the sun tomorrow night, and parachute back to mud-brown earth, umbrella unfolded overhead. Her chuckle will blot out the put-put of the past as its dirty suds swirl down the drain.

Composer and I

There was a piece of paper.

Over time, there have been thousands of pieces of paper—blue, pink, yellow, white, ruled, unruled, marbled, fancily embedded with dried flowers, triangular flap of an envelope, menu bottom, placemat, napkin, matchbook, ticket stub, page of a phone book, rolled, folded, spindled, ripped, crumpled, mutilated, laundered, tacked, taped, pinned, sticky-stuffed, magneted, on the fridge, bulletin board, medicine cabinet, strewn about, piled up, tucked in books, journals, magazines, notebooks, pockets, knapsacks, daypacks, and the occasional glove compartment. At any given moment, there are hundreds, swamping the desk. They've all had things written on them, some by me, most by Composer, and I've been bound to keep them all.

Last week, there was just such a piece of paper—the torn-off top of the front page of the May Day edition of the newspaper, if I remember correctly. Under the jagged baby newsprint teeth ran the small headline that runs above the large headline of the paper that American intellectuals read when we come to live in France, *Le Temps.* I know the small headline read: *Le Pen Hijacks Labor Day for Joan of Arc.* I think a notice in the corner indicated that on page five, the reader would find an analysis of the failure of the Communist Party to pose a challenge to Le Pen. The large headline that day must have concerned the presidential elections in which the arch-conservative nationalist had, in the first round two weeks ago, won a surprise victory, which determined that he would be going on to the second and final round, which took place today. Or perhaps there was a front-page photo of the demonstrations against him, which were many and large on the 1st of May. And I believe there was, on this same piece of newspaper, in my handwriting, a time and a place. Other than that, it was, and is, a harmless shred of paper. Unless the wrong person finds it, like the police, or Composer. Or the right person doesn't, in this case, me or Oona.

The piece of paper may be lost. In any case, I haven't been able to find it yet. It was just another slip of paper—the nearest scrap, receipt, gum wrapper, remittance stub, circular, back of someone else's business card, outdated train schedule. Such a slip of paper might have written on it, for example: *What is cotton candy a metaphor for?* Such a slip of paper is usually grabbed, along with a pen, in a moment of inspiration. Oh never mind. There's no need to wake Composer. It could be a nice quiet night, now that Composer has fallen asleep. Just me and Oona.

An hour ago, we were listening to medieval music, recorded in the thirteenth century in the Mont-Saint-Michel Abbey. We were making love
to the strains of the olden-days, which conjured up monks scurrying under the eaves, hiding in their habits, hustling their manuscripts hither and thither under cover of darkness, felt-shod feet on cobbles, hunger gnawing not in their stomachs but in their quill-pricked, ink-bespattered fingers itching to inscribe the Word in all its glorious embodiments, words that

Suddenly, I noticed that Oona was sitting up smoking a cigarette, not looking too happy, as though waiting for something. Me, I guess. I must have gotten lost.

–What happened? I asked.

–Go, she said.

–Go where?

—Go write it down, she said. But while you're out there

While I'm out here, I should be turning everything upside down again trying to find that piece of paper, that all-important piece of paper, but I'm a sorry bastard; once again, Composer takes the fur-lined seat in the sleigh. I could stand here all night, five floors up, counting chimneypots in the moonlight, but Composer whips me like a husky, bellowing *mush mush*, as we tear across tundras of typeface, kicking up clods of prose, ice crystals of sound. I say, *No, Composer, you are not the boss of me*. But Composer cackles and whips me again. Much is trod upon, and much is lost. Among other things, I lost the end of Oona's last sentence.

In order to lull Composer back to sleep, I begin to copy into the computer what's written in the margins of the brochure from the Mont-Saint-Michel Abbey: my own—or rather, Composer's—jottings. Mont-Saint-Michel was the *pièce de résistance* of our weekend, as it is of the *département* of Ille-et-Vilaine, if not all of Brittany. Next to the short printed version of the history and architecture of it squatting up to its stones in the changing tide, I accumulated three thoughts and several phrases. All things being equal, I average about two thoughts and five phrases or titles a day, but things are never equal, depending on Composer. Mont-Saint-Michel, in particular, is unequalable; Oona likewise.

Oona and I wanted to see Mont-Saint-Michel because Cézanne famously painted it. We pulled into the overflow parking lot along with thousands of other cars, lined up and locked, little cars, sedans, and RVs. Oona observed that it was like going to a rock concert. Could the phalanx fifteen people wide walking down the long road in the fog really be trudging to the site of a painting? Even a series of paintings? The fog seemed right, but could art history really account for the crowds, the young and old, backpack hanging off some part of each person, except us?

—More like a pilgrimage, Oona said.

Indeed. It was taking more than twenty minutes for the unending stream of us to walk from the parking lot to the attraction.

—I think it's something religious, she said.

Then the sun began to burn the fog off a curling infinitude of turrets and alleys, a thousand-year-old sand castle made of stone. Something beyond religious, well into mystical.

—Hold on, I said. I have to write something down. I frisked myself for a pen. The pilgrim behind me rear-ended me. If you're going to stop suddenly and stand still, you have to get out of the flow of traffic.

—Jesus, said Oona. Here, really?

If you could call a built structure a prayer, this one is, this little island in

Shit, Composer was onto it and into the fray. It was a race between me and Composer. I couldn't find anything to write on. I would lose. I tried to store my phrase and my idea until I had some paper to write on, but by the time we had exchanged euros for entry, and received a brochure about the history and architecture of Mont-Saint-Michel

Which is a small stone mountain reaching its fingers and arms up to the heavens in praise, and in the desire to receive the unladeable weight of the almighty in the spirit of the suspension of stone, to meet said spirit with that of the ocean, to transcend the fickle cycle of the tide. On foggy mornings, the rock and abbey pour out of the sky, down into the salt flat marshes off the Baie du Same Name. It is often an island unto itself, every six hours striking out on its own, only to join once more, when the tide waxes nigh, its clerical denizens with that dubious chain of human being that leads to town, to life in the lowly marketplace, and thence to hell, whence

That's how easy it is to wake up Composer. I would have Composer sleep while Composer would probably prefer to slumber. It should be pretty easy to tell the difference between us: one talks regular and the other talks like a horse's ass. I was hoping Composer would be out for a while after that interruptus back in bed, but Composer is a terribly light sleeper.

While I'm out here, what I ought to be doing—rather than trying to knock Composer back out—is finding that scrap of newspaper on which I wrote down what Dane told me and Oona, unless I wrote it on the yellow client copy of the last credit card purchase—which was at the florist on Tuesday where and when I bought lilies for Oona.

Dane is Oona's best friend. He and his co-conspirator (whose name we are not to know, for our own good) are professional tree huggers, environmental activists, or ecoterrorists, depending on your point of view. Last Wednesday, Dane came over to ask us a favor. He thought he was about to be picked up for questioning. He might be held for a little while, and he wasn't sure he would be out in time to give a "friend" some important coordinates. Nothing to worry about, but, so, could he just give us some data and would we be willing to convey it to his friend on Monday? He wanted to deliver the information orally (so there would be no evidence in his hand) but he wanted us to write it down (so there would be no mistake). If Dane was released in time, he would call us to say he could take care of it himself after all.

This morning, after three days in Brittany, and before I realized that I couldn't find the piece of paper in question, I sat back down at the desk I love because it holds my tools. For the gardener, so the shed. I sat here in peaceful contemplation of the possibility of writing this week. The best way to keep things quiet right now would be to forego florid descriptions of my workspace or the states of affect associated with it. I generally try to avoid clichés about the calling to a "certain activity" in order not to

From the dew-splashed divinity of a morning just flown in on the wings of the splendorously plumed birds attending the golden-tongued Calliope, the tuneful Euterpe, and Clio, with her sacred scroll, her copious flowing papyrus, prayers in the form of libacious offerings, to be drunk and drunk and, overflowing, to cascade down the chins and necks of the nearly naked goddesses who perform, with artists everywhere, the miracle of co-creation when

Jesus Christ. I have no choice but to introduce Composer.

This is Composer, who fucks up my life.

Terpsichore with her plectrum, not missing any beats.

This is the bane of my existence. Since I was a teenager, I have been afflicted with a narrator who offers—no, imposes—a running commentary on everything I see, hear, smell, touch, taste, feel, or do. This irrepressible composer mediates every last experience—fights with my dad in the great backyard, cityscapes in the dusk, hot sex, backgammon victories, losses in love, brushing my teeth, endlessly driving on roads, and cetera, ad infinitum. Macroscope, microscope, and periscope on the whole damn continuum from ridiculous to sublime. The color of the sun as against the color of the fog, the way the breaking wave resembles toothpaste as it foams, the arc of my hand reaching for my wallet as I go to pay for the flowers—nothing escapes Composer's voiceover.

When I'm not taking dictation from Composer—or looking for yet another piece of paper—I'm writing a novel for the movement. Actually, I didn't originally set out to write about environmentalism. I pulled that out of the hat *tout de suite* when I first met Oona, which was at a table that she and Dane were running at a neighborhood festival in our *quartier*. Their sign said Green Light, in French. I caught sight of the cool back of her hanging the fourth corner of it up on the pole behind their table, her double-jointed silver-bangled arms stretched out, blonde chignon coming unwisped, and I had suddenly, urgently to come up with something before she turned around. I thumbed a couple of pamphlets on the injustice of international property rights laws that put indigenous people in debt to agribiz corporations for replanting their own crops, and the reappropriation of farmland in Zimbabwe. She turned to face me. I said, I'd like to take some of your materials if I could—I'm writing a novel on environmental degradation. You should talk to him, she said, gesturing at Dane. I'm just helping out. You're a writer?

It's a good cause, Oona and I agree on that. And, but, what would I write about otherwise?

Following Le Pen's victory in the first round on April 21, Dane and his friends chose to act quickly. They wanted to capitalize on this moment precisely because the elections, or rather the protests surrounding them, promised to keep the police busy on the streets and, at least temporarily, out of the hair of the environmentalist activists. At least, that's what Oona and I think we remember Dane saying. I definitely remember Dane proposing that we meet his friend at the Café Verdi Monday morning (if we didn't hear from him, Dane, first)—the one with the violins painted on The violin which must be considered in its relation to the viola— does the violin become the viola and does the latter become the cello which in turn becomes the double bass, as a girl becomes a woman, or must one rather consider the violin and the viola in their relationship to other musical instruments, and to non-musical instruments? To villains, to Villon, to Verlaine, to Violette Le Duc, to Vilnya, to Vietnam, and violence. To Vilaine, as in Ille-et-. To pears. To piccolos. To things with strings and things with bows. Horizontal, vertical, and diagonal cross-referencing systems checked and double checked. *Et voilà*

—Don't flake on me now, Dane had said, looking me right in the eye.

—*Quel* command of slang, I had answered. Had I missed something, I wondered.

It's not just Composer. There's someone else here. I heard a shuffle, a bump, something short of a creak. Someone real. I heard a

Not the police, I hope. No, there's no police around. It must be Oona.

Or Terpsichore with her plectrum, not skipping any beats.

No matter what I do, I can't get rid of Composer. Not to be confused with composure, which I lose often enough.

—How did Ngu like your chapter? Oona calls from the bedroom. I prefer for her to call it a chapter. A couple of weeks ago, I'd asked Ngu to read some stuff of mine and comment on it. She's very smart, and she happens to edit a journal. Plus, she offered, sort of, when we first met. Every minute of the last fourteen days that she was not so moved by my genius that she simply had to email me or pick up the phone and say so immediately was another minute that I suffered deeply. When she came over today, Ngu brought along her comments. I go to the threshold of the bedroom to answer Oona.

—She had a hard time with the stuff about Le Pen and the penis and the Palestinian struggle, and other than that she thought the stuff was okay. I knew she wouldn't like the political bits. But the connection to Burroughs, she could see all that.

Oona is not impressed. It's possible to be a little too good sometimes at imitating masculinity. I wonder why she's not out here looking for that piece of paper, but I better not ask her just now.

How we met Ngu is we went to an art opening in the 13th arrondissement. Oona likes to try to touch the art, but me, I thought it was just the sort of hip event I'd rather be able to say I've gone to than actually go to. The sort of thing I have to do once in a while, just for the credibility. Strangers in black, all of them rakish, with either lipstick or savoir faire. I was at the point of wondering if it would seem immature to go for fourths of the wasabi-baked peas, when we were introduced to a saxophonist and his wife. He would have been a real raconteur if he could remember his own anecdotes without asking her, and if he were charming rather than merely fluent. I began by smiling at the rise of inflection that would normally signal time to smile for auditors; I sought to meet the minimum requirements for social face. But then I tested to see if it made a difference. No. So I let my face go slack except when I was chewing my fifth handful of peas. Oona laughed and touched the wife and then touched the art again. Ngu was an editor and her husband was unstintingly dull.

Tonight, from my desk, I can see that Urania has constellated her friends, the stars, to say to me, It's time, fool. Find the piece of paper. And not one of them is winking. I'm getting hungry. I finger the postcard we brought back for Dane: a notoriously wise guy being divinely inspired. Sitting in his drapey garb, notebook open on his left knee, St. Augustine dips his feather in an inkwell that is being deep-throated by a small lion with a curly mane and an absent eye. The saint looks up into the corner of the arch where his inspiration, a modest angel with wings, is carrying a book. They make it look so easy.

On Thursday, when Oona and I went out for our practice run to the Café Verdi, tens of thousands of people were militating in the streets to register an opinion about Le Pen and his program. Oona suggested we join them. The stumping Le Pen did what he does every May 1; rather than celebrate Labor Day with the rest of Europe, he honors Joan of Arc as a symbol of French national

123

resistance to foreign intrusion. We came back from Brittany early because the culture and history of the old must sometimes yield to culture and history in the making. And, besides, we knew the elections—or the people's response to them, depending on your perspective—would jam the traffic and the metro on Sunday, as it had on Labor Day—or Joan of Arc Day—depending on your perspective. While we were gone, Dane must have been picked up for questioning. We knew because he hadn't left a message on our machine.

We had understood, Oona and I, that it—the crucial information on the famous piece of paper—was the time and place that a certain shipment of hazardous waste would be meeting with a certain interruption as it railed its way east from its origin at the 3D Corporation in northeastern France toward Germany, although we couldn't exactly remember what made us think we knew this. Dane is that good. Oona and Dane know each other from school in England, but he is a German national while she is dual British-French. They were lovers before they knew what lovers were for. When they figured it out, they became friends. Orange-haired, skinny, translucent, like a goldfish on stilts. That's Dane. Canny, transluscious, leather laces crisscrossing their way up her succulent calves from her sandals—that's Oona.

The morning after Dane came over, and before we left that afternoon for Brittany, Oona and I decided to do a practice run of the meeting we were to have with Dane's friend if Dane didn't call us. So we took a break and walked out into the hot city. It was unseasonably warm, like
July in April in Paris.

See, that's Composer, because even I know it was already May and Composer can't resist twiddling a cliché. Traces of Labor Day's demonstrations were scattered on the ground and penned on the walls. Oona rolled up her shirtsleeves as far as they would go—she is so sexy. We walked toward the Café Verdi squinting and smoking. A line of white vans was parked along the length of the avenue. Police faces lurked in their dark windows. Oona winked at one.

Oona's a little cozier with the state than I am. For one thing, she's got citizenship. For another, she works for the Ministry of Culture and Communication as an *Inspecteur de la création*, attending shows and writing them up, so the state can review its culture funding programs. It's our only source of income at the moment. She used to write poetry and sometimes she still does, but I don't rib her too much about selling out. Of course, she doesn't see it that way.

The lilies are still going strong.

If we don't find that piece of paper before tomorrow morning, what will happen? I didn't hear him spell it out, but I got the idea that the activists Dane organized would show up at the action, not be met by the hundreds of others that would have been organized by his colleague, and with their insufficient numbers, the train would get them instead of vice versa. Having crushed Dane's contingent, the train would go on to its destination and dump its hazardous load. The ecoterrorists would have lost the battle and Oona would have lost her best friend. I have no choice but to find that piece of paper, pull my little weight for the cause, and for Oona.

How beautiful she is. Oona's clavicle, horizontal evidence of her endoskeleton, bones bowed like a cello. I say this but I say no more. Composer seems to see Oona's body as an open invitation, a neon sign, arrow making its intermittent way around the rectangle, as though there were an opening at the Oona Motel any time, day or night. I would fight him in the old-fashioned way, but it's hard to land a blow and I become afraid that his weapon is mightier than mine. I fear

Oona's clavicle, Oona's clavichord, Oona's well-tempered clavier, Oona's well-tempered cleaver, and her well-tempered cleavage

Oona is better than blonde; Oona is real.

—Is it Composer again? Honey, come back to bed.

Oona is better than real.

This afternoon, at about four pm, Oona and I decided to prepare a tapenade for Ngu. We had invited her over to share the results of the final election; we hoped she'd leave her husband out riffing somewhere. *Tomorrow*, I thought, as I knocked off today. *Tomorrow is when I will straiten the gate.* I think it every day. I turned on the radio to find, first, preliminary election results, and then, jazz.

For years, I struggled with my first novel. I couldn't figure out how to structure it. You could hear me late at night not knowing how. The novel was going to be called *Erasure*. I went to the patisserie. That was before Oona

Music gets to say—and be—Hosanna

Mute letters on a page do not

I rifled through a stack of papers.

—Why don't you just get a notebook, asked Oona. And save us all a lot of trouble.

—Notebooks are for poseurs.

—And for poseuses?

—Posies, I said, pointing to the lilies. Oona finished chopping apples and pears for a compote. I watched her puree the olives.

—Are you determined not to help out here? Oona asked.

—I make sure not to do anything useful. I absolutely eschew utility. What do you eschew, Oona?

—Oona don't eschew no little green apples.

An hour later, Oona served the tapenade, along with some

bread and red wine, to Ngu, who showed up without her meta-phor. Oona and I gave silent praise. Ngu didn't want to talk so much about my work, probably didn't want to leave Oona out of the conversation. She tried to seem more interested in the elections. Chirac had won eighty-two percent of the vote, and that was that for Le Pen. We drank to his defeat. Oona brought in the cheese and the compote.

–How's work? Ngu asked Oona. At last.

–Naturally, I began, it goes slowly. I'm a *mot juste* kind of Mo' juice? Mo' better juice? Or mo' Jews? Like Jewn of Arc? Like the kind Le Pen would probably prefer to pack up and ship out along with all dark people from anywhere, all those whose blood is not *bleu (rouge, blanc et)* with monarchy, empire, and republic piled on medieval stone, the Middle Ages piled under the monarchy but sending up fresh columns of smoke from the eternal French bon-fire like today is all there ever was. Swirls of smoke wrought in iron at the entrance to every metro station, the word *Metro* itself done up modern style. *Moderne* piled on top of metropolitanism, on top of straw and bamboo, on top of large colonies in Africa and Asia. The megatons of stone and the untold intention the way the one hew and the one cry the other into beauty that lives for ages, as though there's no Algeria, never was, as though there's no such thing as desert (only dessert), or desert peoples, as though beauty itself is a function of the temperate zone, cultivated here in a haze of smoke and mirrors and champagne, here where passion safely unfurls itself on foundations of stone and iron, which don't burn even

Ngu was just staring at me; she'd never met Composer. Finally she asked, If it's tapenade, does it have to have olives in it?

–Sure, said Oona. Otherwise, the whole concept has no speci-ficity. Olive Oona so much sometimes.

—So how did you like Mont-Saint-Michel? Ngu asked.

—We loved it, but it doesn't really look the same in the paintings, I said.

—What paintings? Ngu asked.

—You know, Cézanne's series, the ones that launched Post-Impressionism, I said. Ngu almost choked on the tapenade. That was Mont-Saint-*Victoire*. She was somewhere between sniffing and spitting.

—How embarrassing. Just the way that
Presidential candidates like Le Pen foamulate about how foreigners are destroying France, minus the Muslim, Eastern-European or Arab, part. The kind of thing beside which McDonaldization looks like petty crimes against culture and history. Just the kind of thing that makes white French people vote for right-wing foamulators like Le Pen. The very way that

If Ngu said anything, I wouldn't have known it. You see what I live with. I lose whole minutes. Oona came back into the room empty handed. Next time, Oona says, she will invite Ngu along to a play—the Ministry always gives her two tickets. Or maybe they'll go to a chamber concert. It's hard to believe I ever thought Composer was my friend, or better, was proof that I was a writer. In the beginning, I did think Composer was my friend. Once upon a time, I thought Composer was my friend. On a midnight weary, I still thought Composer was my friend. I was in college and I thought I had lots of friends I didn't really have. It wasn't until I hooked up with Oona about three years ago that I began to make real friends. Like Dane and such.

I resume the search.

—Oona, where did you put all that mail? I call.

Ends of sentences, Ngu recommended. Doesn't she believe in beginnings thereof? I hadn't thought her so conventional. I reject her criticism; in the name of realism, I cannot

—I think you put it next to the recycling pile, she responds.

You see what *she* lives with. I hear her reach for something on the table beside the bed. It kills me that I can't find that piece of paper. Dane's going to kill us too.

—What do you mean *us*, American man? asked Oona over dinner. She seemed to be taking the case of the missing piece of paper rather casually.

Suddenly, I thought I heard Melpomene whistling in the stairwell.

—Did you hear that? Oona asked.

—No, I lied.

—Do you think that's Dane? Oona asked.

—I didn't hear anything.

—Exactly. Do you think that's Dane in police custody?

—Oh, I hear it now.

In the Mont-Saint-Michel Abbey, there is a scriptorium, where the medieval writers wrote. In silence. But not in peace. They had the big Composer in the sky tickling their ears. Sometimes I try to think of ways to kill Composer. But how could I take a pick-axe to a disembodied friend, or shoot one in the head? It would be like cutting off my face to spite my nose.

I'm not writing everything I think. Who would want me to do that? Not even the police.

From time to time, Oona reads my work. She always says the same thing, mainly that I should add more pages. She just can't see how ideological that is. I might make the changes Oona recommends. I might not.

What Cage did for music

Oona's just written a poem. While I've been out here getting hungry.

—Want to hear it? she asks. It's short.

THE LETTER OF THE LOVE

the stranger in bed

the stronger in bed

—What are you trying to say? I ask.

—It's just a poem, she says, as though there is something she isn't saying

See how it turns on just one letter, the bedded and the bedder ever wed in epic pleasure where the odd and the unknown outstrippeth that which has familiar grown, and the missive in the sheets, the *a* the *o* she never meets while you munch on the bread you eats instead of getting ever better

—My very own Erato, I say, trying to wrest Composer into silence. There is nothing more embarrassing than Composer in full Thalia regalia.

—Cute, Oona groans.

When I first thought I might want to be a writer, I thought the best way to go about it was to work in a bookstore. Maybe a book would get written by me abracadabra, like studying for an exam by sleeping with the textbook under your pillow. Certain illusions I am still under thirty years later. For example, the illusion that those little scraps of paper have something to do with writing. Talent or talents, one or thirty, *the* Individual, flaming, Arnoldian, or otherwise true inborn native genius, cannot be bought, bartered, traded, or exchanged, and if you sold your soul, your son, your stock, or your sneakers for some, I'm sorry to tell you, you were scammed.

On the brochure, there is the printed matter about the history and architecture of Mont-Saint-Michel, and on the back page, in my writing, a question sideways up the length of the margin of print: *What is cotton candy a metaphor for?*

One of the lilies is starting to droop.

I would be the kind of writer who

—What are you doing? Oona calls froggily from the bedroom. She finished her report after dinner, and before we went to bed, which was before Composer acted up and drove me to the computer. Now Oona is beginning to sound sleepy, and soon she will sleep the sleep of the just.

I am now panicking. I beg Oona not to abandon me, to get out of bed and come search with me.

—How about a ritual invocation of Mnemosyne? Oona suggests.

—The mother of all muses? I protest. There is no way to do that without Composer getting into the act.

—At least Composer works hard, Oona says. I know this is the most suspectly capitalist of values, she goes on, but you must admit that Composer is prolific, unlike certain writers who will go unnamed. Composer puts out.

Ouch. Now I'm put out.

—What are you saying?

—Nothing, it's just an observation.

I kiss her.

—We are all a lost piece of paper, she says, as I head back out of the bedroom. Now who's being cute. I don't know how she can sleep at a moment like this. I need to go for a walk, maybe search out a little dessert at the late-night place at the Bastille. There's only one cure for the mounting panic.

—I'm going out, I say to Oona. I may have dropped the piece of paper on the stairs or in the courtyard or left it at the patisserie. I think I'll stop in and ask. She would laugh but she is more than half asleep.

Maybe Oona is onto something. Composer does write a lot.

It's terrible stuff, but it exists. Maybe I should take a page from Composer's book. I could write about Composer and all the pieces of paper. God knows I've got enough notes for *A La Recherche du Temps Perdu*. I could go back to the transcriptions of all the old notes and revise them until they're readable, go back into the extensive Composer archives and use Composer's own compositions to turn the tables. That could take a lifetime. But what else have I got?

The Communists are holding a party at the Bastille, huge speakers on trucks, blaring and sharing the musical wealth, very fine filaments of rain, a definite relief from the political and climatological tension of the last two weeks. Up on the monument, there, some kids. Some of the same kids, perhaps, who last week demonstrated here and wrote on the monument, assuming it unto themselves as a public space that would accommodate speech, that would receive and reflect a message to the motherland, in extra tall and large graffiti, the most visible of which said *Fuck Le Pen* (in the very English despised as the tongue of the cultural imperialist, not to mention the political and economic members of the same species, which nonetheless *se parle partout*). It has the unmistakable mark of Clio backdropping a modern dance. The kids are young, vaguely punky, androgynous, at least from a distance; the monument is shrouded in smoke, and up on the massive elevated foot of it, one young person holds a blazing pink fireball, a big cotton candy licked by so many small tongues of flame, whence issues the smoke. Through the haze, through the crackling light at midnight, Le Pen's campaign burns at the stake of *liberté*. Another young person waves the *tricolore* out in front of a row of triumphant youth marching their hips in time to the music, happy and proud, as though they have no less than reclaimed France. Indeed, it is *Liberty*

Leading the People straight out of the canvas and into three dimensions: the flag, the people, and the secure possession of the future. How do they preserve, the rioting kids organized under the banner whose very being is posited in opposition to the state, that warm fuzzy feeling, that sense of possession, of the ever-loving bloody *République*, so that in their smoke-besotted minds, the victory today was a national one and, at one and the same time, was theirs. Just outside the frame of the picture that refers to, if it does not replicate, the painting—by Delacroix, for sure—comes a figure whose march parallels that of the punk Liberty undulating on the monument, only down on the ground and thus walking, closer and closer, a red-haired stick figure, looking suspiciously like Dane.

That's so Composer. But wait a minute, Composer is right. It is Dane. Oh, thank God he's not in jail. Why didn't he call and let us off the hook? I'm going to kill him.

–Well, fancy that, looks like you're free.

–Of course I am. I called this afternoon to say so—didn't Oona tell you? Dane claps a broad pink palm on my shoulder in a gesture of *fraternité*.

Retrospectively, Oona comes back into the room where Ngu's eyebrows are suspended in surprised sufferance. Retroauditorially, I am leaving 'off a speech about French xenophobia, under which there has been the sound of the phone ringing, Oona's voice, conspiratorial laughter, all from the other room. Now I retrieve this information and I understand that Oona has been playing with my mind. Trying to make some kind of point?

–Oh, that's right—I guess she did mention it. Hey, want to go for a pastry and a cup of

–I'd like to, he says. But I've got a meeting.

–Good luck, I say, as Dane slips off into the crowd to conspire, leaving me to my own devices.

Oona must be very tired of me hiding behind Composer or she would not have done something so off-pissing.

Composer is right? Did I really just think that? Can I quote myself? But why would I? Then again, whom else would I quote?

At the Café Français a couple of minutes later, as I reach into my pocket for euros to pay for my Napoleon, I find a piece of paper. It says *I and I*. Composer's idea of a title. Not a bad start for my table-turning project, now that I think of it. Maybe I'll leave off with the environmental-novel-that-couldn't to turn over this particular new leaf—and not tell Oona! The waiter will bring the pastry and an espresso to my favorite table by the window. I pat myself down for something to write with, and look back up to see Oona sitting at our habitual spot. It's a good thing she's so pretty, all rumpled and sleepish.

—Are you looking for le pen? Oona asks, brandishing a ballpoint, and smiling—sheepishly, unless I'm projecting.

—In fact, I've got just le paper to go with it, I say.

They Come From Mars

They come from Mars From Mars they come Mars they come from
Come from Mars they Mars they come from They come from Mars
From Mars they come They come from Mars Come from Mars they
Mars they come from Come from Mars they From Mars they come

They from Mars come They come from ther upon ther ship Ther
ship from Mars land like star shot down like star shot down
Next hour next ship shot fall land like star shot down Hour
upon hour more ship from Mars fall down They land ther ship

They park ther ship down town They dont obey ship park regs
Even when City Hall says dont they park ther ship ther Then
them folk from Mars exit ther ship THER UGLY Thru open ship
door flow folk from Mars Next ship next door more folk flow

Thru ship door flow flow flow UGLY UGLY Cant tell sure seem
like they have more legs than dogs nine legs Seem like they
have nine ears nine eyes nine lips Ugly mugs Seem like they
must have more life than cats Like cats like dogs they stra

nger here Like fish they emit foul odor What Home upon Mars
dont they wash Garb also very ugly Here come folk from ship
from Mars with many limb with ugly mugs mite have tiny geni
tals prob ably have huge geni tals Seem sexu ally fear some
some hows plus they play some noys some long away stra song

Then they walk pour flow ooze down town Rows upon rows flow
folk from Mars rows upon rows like ants Dont obey when City
Hall says dont Then wewe spec they want fear they want TAKE
OVER TAKE OVER Wewe spec fear that what they want they want
from usus Come from Mars this flow ants that want what wewe
have rite here What Dont Mars have nice down town nice life

Ever morn ings ever days more ship park down town more folk
from Mars flow into ours park down ours road into ours skoo
yard Mart ians seem like want ours flip pant food ours free
less sons even ours dust What wors they want ours stuf Want
ands want ands want ands want Want ours home ours blue burb
trak hows What dont they have nice huts over thar Mars Must
they come here with them want want ways What dont they want

Keep your door shut Even more lock bolt nail down your door
when they howl from your lawn howl with echo echo dust from
Mars Then stay more than five feet away from your door They
will meow like cats meow like moon dust echo They will chow
your food They will soil your rugs They will reek rank foul
They will peer into your john They cant help such acts They
dont know good from evil rite from rung They have idea from
Mars that they will come take your dust your stuf take over

your very life Well they wont they cant Dont able them Hide
your dust your food your less sons Hide your stuf away Hide
your very body your hole self Even when they seem nice dont
talk with them tall cost Vote them away Dont just vote Call
City Hall Tell City Hall send them away Call Gove rnor Dont
just call Sing more loud Also load your guns Wewe spec that
Mars folk will take your guns turn them roun hunt your good
life ther fore dont give dont sell them guns BANG Wait List
ento that noys Soun like they miss Mars That dont make sens

Miss they Mars If in case they miss Mars EASY They must away
from here ship back home Mars Mars take sits name from rage
full gods ring road near Merc suns baby Mars with that hard
warr iors bada ssfu ckyu bull like bell iger ence wher them
folk gets ther ways ther rant rail rave want want want ways
Wher they gets ther hows Wher they gets ther idea that they
want what wewe have Wher they make ther veni vidi vici ship
from Venu shot ship dust Ther will Wher they bord ship weep
bord ship weep such weep baby cant wail more than they Star
sail weep What have wewe here Whyd oMar tian come then sing
such song upon arri ving stra song from loin lame ntay tion
Fuck that moon dust noys Dont know bout yous but I ands mine

will keep them from move next door what ever wewe have todo
What ever wewe have todo make Mart ians stop talk Mart ians
talk walk Mart ians walk nolo nger make moon dust meal reek
alll over town nolo nger hawk moon dust inna play grou Wewe
hear this news read that Blok chrt that graf more data ever
kind pruf with outa dout Mart ians take drug comm itcr imes
Wewe talk inga bout drug sand crim tear inga part ours burb
Hate most ofal that keen that wine that song that soun like
baby lost ther mama papa Make wewe want toto rend ourg arme
ntsS hutu pNOW Wewe will rend ther Mart ians garm ents covr
over ther head with ther mult iple ante nnae once andf oral
fore plur ibus unum Wewe usun them Wewe goan bind them hush
them muff lest ifle ther tune that soun like bird flew time
gone that make wewe want toun bury Gram pa!! STOP !!It hurt
Else wewe stop that moon dust bull shit fory ouch ange your
laym asss tune Wewe doit rite pass laws then dont wait long
forn olaw stop asss hoot earm uffs offy ours nine time each
Mart ians ifwe have toto conv ince Mart ians ther snop lace
like home ther snop lace like home ther snop lace like moon
dust home away from Mars Goan take with them that song that
soun Cant quit plac itso fami liar What part fear muff dont
they unde stan Gone make them sari they were ever year afta
year ning tobr eath free from Mars Weve kill mens four less
faut wars four more year inye arou tNow wewe gone bust usus
some head four post erit yfor Momf orju stfo rfun buts till
that pain that OUCH ears what skil ling usis that song that
bloo dyso ngNO MORE that moon dust song that just wont die

Please Compose Your Photographs More Carefully

Dear Editor,

I'm writing on a subject of great importance, which concerns the composition of photographs, mostly pictures of people. I read your paper every day, and on Sundays, so I am hoping that you will alert your readers to something that many might suffer from, namely, if you can't see someone's limbs or other body parts in a certain photograph, you can't assume they're there in reality. Although I have seen this problem in action all my life, I am finally speaking out after sixty years of silence, inspired by your story last week on landmines in Bosnia. As you have written about before, there are mines lying in wait all over the globe. Meanwhile, on the domestic front, well-intentioned readers may carelessly commit the same acts as mines, cutting off body parts of innocent people, just by taking photographs without a thought to their composition, sometimes going so far as to inadvertently make orphans out of little babies.

I connect this with the fact that "One is not born an amputee but rather becomes one," which I read somewhere, not in your paper, if I may say so without causing offense. That means that behind every amputation there is an event. Usually not, but sometimes, planned. Usually not wanted. Usually sudden and surprising, usually violent, usually bloody. That's part of the trouble, the foreshortened end of a limb is associated in the mind with a really bad thing happening.

I'll give you an illustration of what I'm talking about from a picture I have always had right here at home: three mid-century women, looking very familiar, all smiling broadly. Two squeezed together in a low-backed armchair with chintz upholstery, the third sitting on the floor between them, the trio of them scrunched together to all fit in the picture. Bouffant lampshade on the end-table beside them, fire pokers in the style of the time just visible leaning against the fireplace not pictured here. One of the ones on the chair, the only blonde among them, seems to be legless. Her legs are probably just squinched behind the back of the floor-sitting one, but they might not be. And you can't see a left arm on the blonde one. You do not know for sure that this woman has anything other than a head, half a torso, and a right arm. Her brave smile stretched so wide as to make her squint, she makes it look like that's enough. But even if it was enough then, it wasn't later on that same year of the photo. There is evidence of what I'm saying, also not pictured here. I'm trying to be objective, like your reporters, but it's hard because I know two of the women in the picture. The third one, the blonde, squinting so you don't even know if she has eyes, was my mother.

The photograph in question is very badly composed so that the lap and legs of the woman sitting on the floor are cut off, in addition to the right hand she has placed on them. Also cut off are the two feet of the one on the chair whose legs you *can* see, Aunt Glad. That one is the luckiest, she definitely has everything except her feet. Of course, I know Aunt Glad and I've seen she has feet. The one on the floor might have no lower half and no right hand, but is that better or worse than maybe having no legs and no left arm? Anyway, that's Aunt Susan and I've seen her whole legs and right arm too, missing in the photo but, in fact, stuck on her now like always. Also what you can't see of the smiling blonde woman is if she worried sometimes, which judging by what happened she must have. Amputations after all come in many shapes and sizes.

Like in that story you wrote about Sierra Leone, in 1999, where you say, "As many as 4,000 men women and children suffered mutilation, crude amputations of their hands, arms, legs, lips or ears... men who refused to rape members of their own families had their limbs amputated as punishment." You had a photo spread along with this story, so I know it's real, people with all kinds of things cut off. What an ingenious punishment if leaving people living but broken is what you're after. Life without lips, it breaks my heart. What you don't see in the photos is them living with that machete forever.

Here's another thing. In a way, it doesn't even matter if a person is a genuine amputee or not, because if people think she is, they treat her like one whether they're right or wrong. Say I'm at the bus depot and I'm leaning back against the railing of the stall of my bus. I've got my left leg tucked up behind me, toe hooked on the rail. To all the world, it looks like I have no left leg from the knee down. In a flash, I have been taken for having a missing leg. Or my companion bends down to get a magazine out of the bag at my feet and blocks my legs from view. To fellow travelers who don't know me, I might not have those legs. You yourself might seem to be an amputee to someone some day and then you'll know what it feels like. And if your readers don't believe me, later on, when they're done with the paper, they should go look through their old cardboard box of photos, flip through some old albums with the tired adhesive, see how vulnerable they are.

But then again, this should give everyone the opportunity to empathize. To see that amputation should not be held against the amputee; it's nothing they did wrong, sometimes nothing they did at all. Just like babies born out of wedlock. Those women in that picture—they are just having a good time. They are basically innocent. They are waiting for special friends and husbands-to-be away at war, on business, at school. At war. One of whom will not come home. Popcorn pops just outside of the picture. Morning glories peak in the window box and begin to fade.

I read in your *Sunday Digest* that ancient warriors commonly sought vengeance by cutting off the noses of the enemy with a saber, as proved in 1992 when Japan—to right a historical wrong—returned twenty thousand noses that its army had amputated from Korean soldiers and civilians during a military invasion in 1597. The noses, along with some heads of Korean generals, had been preserved in a special memorial for nearly four hundred years. A vault or a sarcophagus made of dark and veiny stone, here I speculate, polished by generations of uniformed young men with bad eyesight or flat feet.

When the picture I'm talking about took place, we lived in a red brick building in Morgantown, three stories of apartments, two on each side, white trim, symmetrical, windows, window boxes with blue flowers, everything. Endtables, sidearms, fire pokers. All of us. My mother, Elaine, who I'm told really did have feet, and her two sisters, Aunt Susan and Aunt Glad with all their parts intact, who told me so, when they thought I was old enough to understand. Just outside the picture, a baby bassinet with a baby in it. I still have a piece of pink satin from the ribbing I've worried near to tatters trying to get the stain off. Burning a hole in the mailbox outside the apartment with the chintz chair, the unopened letter from the government inviting my mother to come and retrieve my father's belongings, and then they present her with a medal that still gleams over all this time.

Meanwhile, going back to Bosnia again, your latest *Digest* offers this human interest update: children running and jumping in fields trip mines. The children trip and they fall to the ground, never to get up again the same, because when the mines explode they explode little legs and arms. Even though the war is supposedly over. Although it was illegal for the criminal of war to have laid those mines without making a map in the first place. And even if they gave the maps they don't make to the children playing, it wouldn't help because in between the laying and the tripping, the rains come and wash the mines partway across the field, partway down the hill, some distance from where they were laid in the first place. Now that they can't play anymore, except with their mouths, the children are only too happy to pose for the camera, or they don't have anything better they can do. You show the nice Belgian doctor stretching the long arm of aid to help the children and round them up for the journalist.

When you cut off someone's arms, even soccer isn't the same. Think about it.

Who took this old picture of the three women? Not me. I was too young. What took my mother away, so long ago? Her own hand, they told me. I don't like to think about where her various parts are now because they are not preserved in any memorial, like those noses were, like my father is, and because they will not be recomposed or returned to me in a future act of restitution. Singe of sulfur forever.

One thing when you are a newspaper covering a real situation. But to your readers at home: I urge people to please compose your photographs more carefully. It is not easy for amputees in this world. They don't want your pity, but don't make things harder for them. Bad enough what's missing. A picture is worth a thousand words, so think about that when you take a picture and don't act like a butcher. So people like me don't have to worry about unnecessary amputations and their silent victims, which are, so often it's practically ironic, family and friends. Meanwhile, viewers of photographs, including me, should probably not always jump to conclusions.

Signed,
Mine Eyes

So What Elapses?

Bubble up words to affix to the fact that she can't don't won't love me any more. Or is it I who won't love her. Please bubble up words I say to the tv to the radio to the magazines full of them, but poetry seeps into the carpet, not to be picked up again, not with the nimblest of fingers, can't be reread, can't be reattracted ionically though I meet it with tears, and don't reabsorb though I lay my terry head down. Poetry dries stainlessly. So I'm down to *shit fuck* and words like *tears*. I'm down to doing the laundry which overflows my empty arms and I slip, stumble, fall, and hit my knee on the sofa that is empty of cats; a sock jumps, chasing the poetry into the rug. I bend down to pick up the sock and in so doing drop the pillow case where she used to lay her head. Fuck shit slapstick.

On my way down to the basement, I make sure, out of habit, to close the door so that the cats won't escape. Then I remember that they're dead; they can't escape.

First they peed wherever their ailing little organs let loose, usually the rug, and now vamoose, they're lost to where pets go, I don't know, maybe down a chute. Kidney failure killed them both, first one then the other, and now the symbolism's going to get them eight more times. Oh sweet furry kitties cuddling for years, I'm sorry. There where you sat seated on me, my thighs your bed, it's empty now.

Downstairs the metal buttons on who knows whose jeans those were in the first place clank again and again and again and again. It's on the tip of my tongue, the hook on which to hang my shit fuck I have to say *heart*. Maybe poetry can be drunk. If I have to, I will suck at the rug, find words. Finally I find one: *elapse*. I have sucked too long to think I will find another any time soon, so I pat, scratch, and tickle this one, hold it on my lap. Clank.

She can't don't won't come sit by me and play with words any more, or it is I.

So what elapses? What else besides time? Clank. Just curses and sighs?

I mean I mean I mean I mean, we all know what *collapses*—World Trade Towers into which planes have flown, sections of Highway 580 after an earthquake, the Igo-Pruitt housing complex when detonated from the inside, the Ottoman empire, and economies. Clank. Likewise, we know what *relapses*—alcoholism, among other habits, convalescents, and stocks. Clank. And we know what simply *lapses*—memberships to gyms, subscriptions to unsatisfying magazines, one's Catholicism of origin, certain rights of possession under certain conditions, Adam and Eve, and memory. Clank. Thus *lapse* seems like relax, let go, go slack, subside; *collapse* is do it all with her; *relapse* would be do all that shit again. Clank.

.

The cats elapsed.

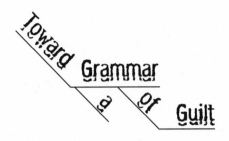

Toward a Grammar of Guilt

11.

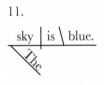

sky | is \ blue.
The

111.

I | pay | taxes
year. my
every

1V.

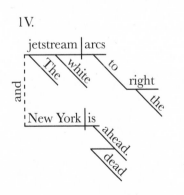

jetstream | arcs
The white to
right
the
and
New York | is
ahead.
dead

V.

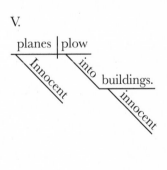

planes | plow
Innocent into
buildings.
innocent

147

V1.

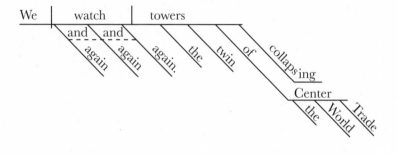

....

V11.

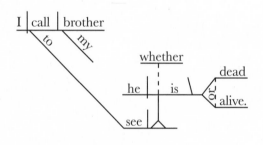

....

V111.

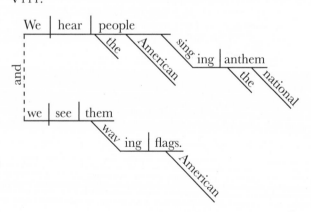

148

1X.

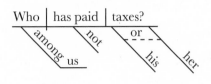

....

X.

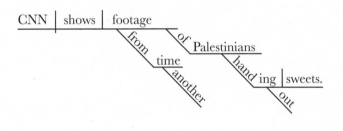

....

X1.

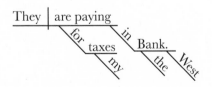

X11.

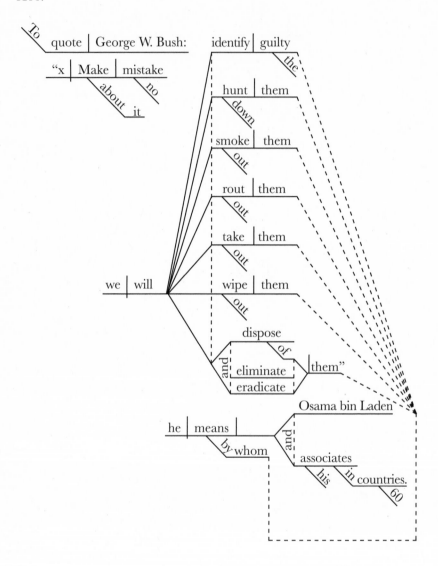

150

X111.

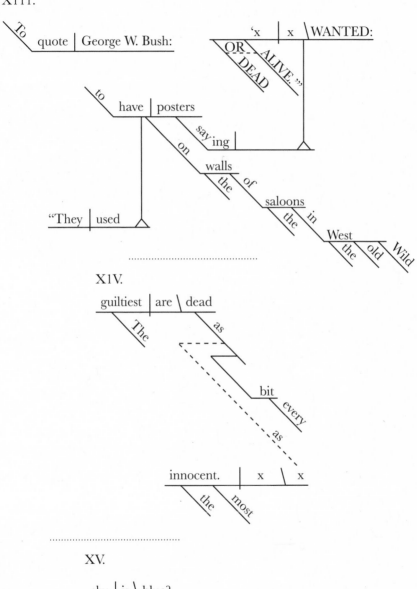

To quote | George W. Bush:

'x | x \ WANTED:
OR ALIVE. " DEAD

to have | posters
saying |
on walls
the of
saloons
the in
West
the old Wild

"They | used

....

X1V.

guiltiest | are \ dead
The
as

bit
every
as

innocent. | x \ x
the most

....

XV.

sky | is \ blue?
the Why

151

XV1.

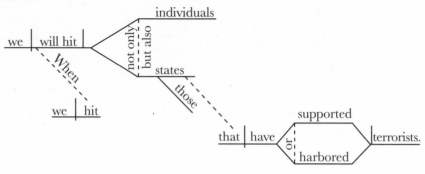

XV11.

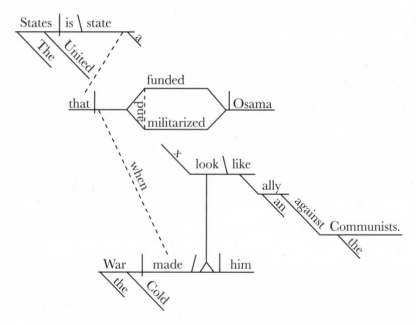

XV111.

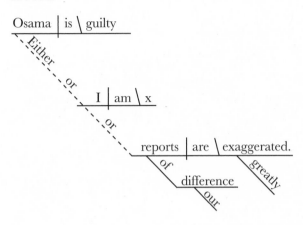

X 1X.

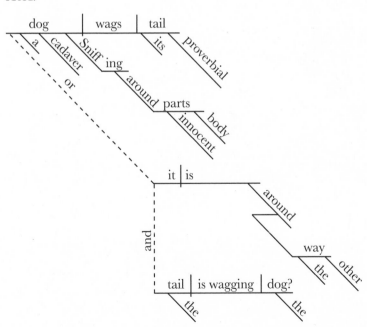

153

XX.

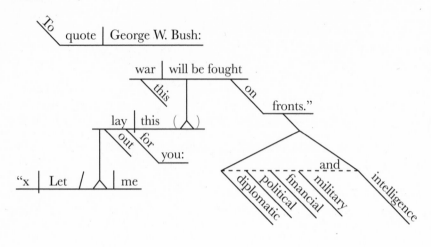

....

XX1.

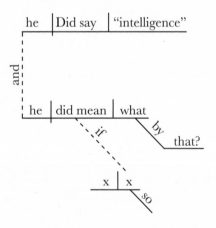

XX11.

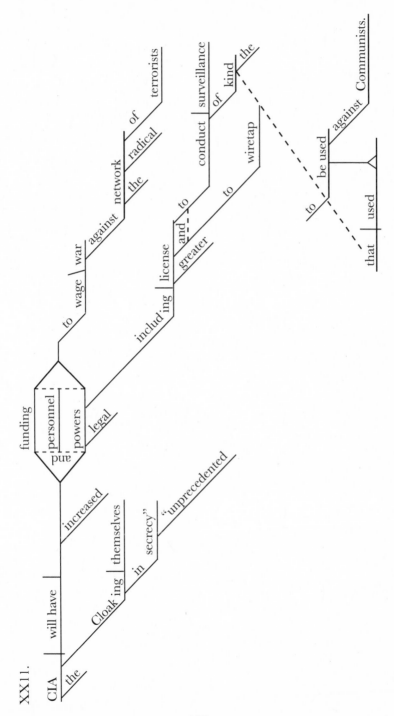

155

XX111.

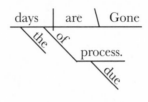

days | are \ Gone
the / of / process. due

....

XX1V.

CIA | will be changing | name.
The / soon / your

....

XXV.

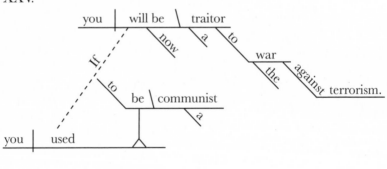

you | will be \ traitor
If / now / a / to
war / the / against terrorism.
you | used / to / be \ communist / a

....

XXV1.

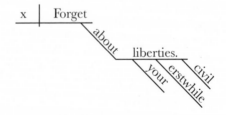

x | Forget
about / liberties.
your / erstwhile / civil

XXV11.

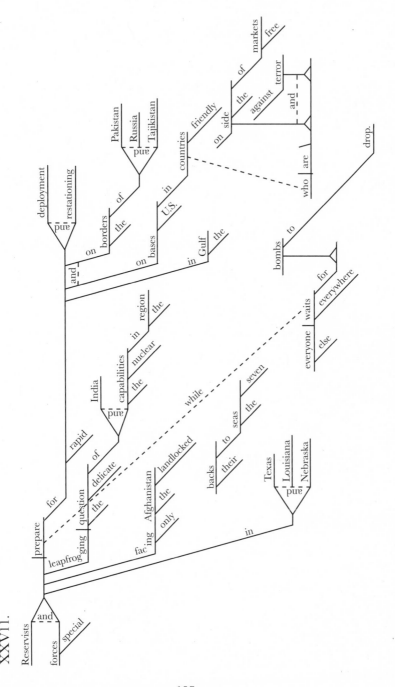

XXV111.

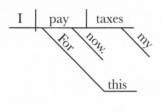

....

XX1X.

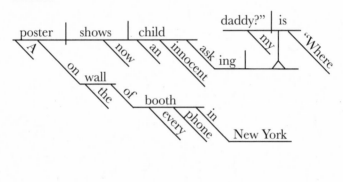

....

XXX.

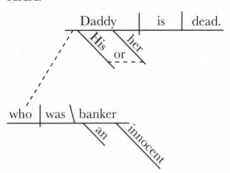

XXX1.

Who | can show | line

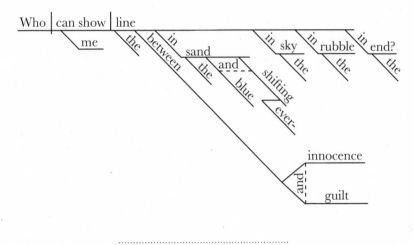

XXX11.

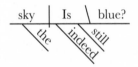

XXX111.

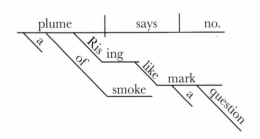

159

11.   The sky is blue.

111.   I pay my taxes every year.

1V.   The white jetstream arcs to the right and New York is dead ahead.

V.   Innocent planes plow into innocent buildings.

V1.   We watch the twin towers of the World Trade Center collapsing again and again and again.

V11.   I call my brother to see whether he is dead or alive.

V111.   We hear the American people singing the national anthem and we see them waving American flags.

1X.   Who among us has not paid his or her taxes?

X.   CNN shows footage from another time of Palestinians handing out sweets.

X1.   They are paying for my taxes in the West Bank.

X11.   To quote George W. Bush: "Make no mistake about it, we will identify the guilty, hunt them down, smoke them out, rout them out, take them out, wipe them out, dispose of, eliminate, and eradicate them," by whom he means Osama bin Laden and his associates in 60 countries.

X111.   To quote George W. Bush: "They used to have posters on the walls of the saloons in the old Wild West saying 'WANTED: DEAD OR ALIVE.'"

X1V.   The guiltiest are every bit as dead as the most innocent.

XV.   Why is the sky blue?

XV1.   When we hit, we will hit not only individuals, but also those states that have supported or harbored terrorists.

XV11.   The United States is a state that funded and militarized Osama when the Cold War made him look like an ally against the Communists.

XV111. Either Osama is guilty or I am or reports of our difference are greatly exaggerated.

X1X.   Sniffing around innocent body parts, a cadaver dog wags its proverbial tail, or is it the other way around and the tail is wagging the dog?

XX.　　To quote George W. Bush: "Let me lay this out for you: this war will be fought on diplomatic, political, financial, military, and intelligence fronts."

XXI.　　Did he say "intelligence," and if so, what did he mean by that?

XXII.　Cloaking themselves in "unprecedented secrecy," the CIA will have increased funding, personnel, and legal powers to wage war against the radical network of terrorists, including greater license to wiretap, and to conduct surveillance of the kind that used to be used against Communists.

XXIII.　Gone are the days of due process.

XXIV.　The CIA will soon be changing your name.

XXV.　If you used to be a communist, you will now be a traitor to the war against terrorism.

XXVI.　Forget about your erstwhile civil liberties.

XXVII.　Reservists and special forces in Texas, Louisiana, and Nebraska prepare for rapid deployment and restationing in the Gulf, on U.S. bases in friendly countries who are on the side of free markets and against terror, and on the borders of Pakistan, Russia, and Tajikistan, their backs to the seven seas, facing only the landlocked Afghanistan, leapfrogging the delicate question of India and the nuclear capabilities in the region, while everyone else everywhere waits for bombs to drop.

XXVIII.　For this, I pay my taxes now.

XXIX.　A poster on the wall of every phone booth in New York now shows an innocent child asking: "Where is my Daddy?"

XXX.　His or her Daddy, who was an innocent banker, is dead.

XXXI.　Who can show me the line between innocence and guilt in the blue and ever-shifting sand, in the sky, in the rubble, in the end?

XXXII.　Is the sky indeed still blue?

XXXIII.　Rising like a question mark, a plume of smoke says no.

Seven Indexes

FIRST: Index of First Lines

A long time ago, I cut my teeth on poets. That was then. I fuck
                        all kinds of people on the Q train
Authorize. Barbary. Carburize. Daedalus. Elegy. Fenderbend.

B. was the eldest of three children, disliked butter, liked Swed-
Because she has a long O sound in each of her three names (if
Bubble up words to affix to the fact that she can't don't won't love

Dear Editor,

I began as we all do by wanting something, but I hardly knew
I would like seduction without commitment; dubious intentions;

Madly. More madly. Potatoes. More madly than that.

N OUESU BUT. N OUESU BUT EAR OUESU BUT.

Reader, if you're looking for someone who missed you and

The kids across the street spend a hell of a lot of time running
The sky is blue. I pay taxes.

There was a piece of paper.
They come from Mars From Mars they come Mars they come from

You're in your first year of college in the North, where you've

SECOND: Index of Proper Names

THIRD: Index

of a jockey,	bowlegs, corduroys, gaiters, and a jacket
of a particular geographic place or social group,	a particular pronunciation of a word
of a predator, for a monkey,	a certain alarm by a member of its own species
of a sailor,	a rolling gait
of a sexually receptive member of its own species, for some insects,	the sense of a pheromone downwind
of a shot,	a piece of mould with a bullet hole in it
of an animal's physical impairment,	a limping gait
of displeasure or concern to a human,	a scowling facial expression
of impending rain,	dark clouds in the west
of rain falling now,	a low barometer
of something considerable happening,	a tremendous thunderbolt
of the availability of food or a shock to follow, in an animal behavior experiment,	a flashing light
of the cookies' readiness to be removed from the oven,	a beep
of the direction of warmer water, for a fish in the sea,	the direction of greater light
of the imperative to stop your car or incur risk,	a red light
of the time of day,	a sundial or a clock
of the vertical direction,	a plumb bob

FOURTH: in publishing, a guide to the contents of a book, publication, or multimedia collection, designed to help the reader more quickly and easily find information; not simply a list of the major terms in a publication, an organized map of the contents of a book, arranged to make the contents clearly visible and comprehensible to the reader; an alphabetical listing of names and topics along with

**FIFTH: that part of the glove that covers
"that finger"**

Body part(s) accent ankle antennae **arm(s)**
                              double-jointed
                              left
                              of B.'s unending review
                              right
                              unbeatable
ass
  horse's
back(s) belly blood
                red running
bones braid brain breast(s) breath calves cheekbones cheek(s) chest
                                                      wound in
chignon chin chops, licked cilium **cilia** clavicle cleavage cock
concordance: an index of all main words in a book along with their immediate
  contexts
corpuscul(ar) crotch cunt curly gates dimple ear(s) eggs elbow(s)
endoskeleton expression, facial
                grin
                sneer
                squint
eye(s)
  Mine
  my
eyebrows eyelashes forearms face(s) faceless fallopian tubes feet
                                              felt-shod
                                            flat
finger(s)
  index
  ink-bespattered
  leafless
  quill-pricked
fingernails fist flagella flesh foot, of the monument genitals glands goatee
half, lower **hair**
                dreads
                dark-haired
                facial
                of the environmental activists
                ever-nerveless
hairless **hand(s)**
          by her own

index
in one
iron
missing
on
right
head(s)
cocked
heart
tattered
ticker
hip(s) huevos intestines kidneys knee(s)
bended
bringing to its
lap **leg(s)**
left
of trip
legless limb(s) lip(s) liver lung mane midriff mouth muscle(s)
abs
delts
index extensor
pecs
quad
mugs nap(s) neck(s) nerve(s) nipples noggin nose(s) organ(s) palm
penis pulse pussy rib rib cage sap scabs shoulder(s) shins sides skeleton(s)
index
skin smile spume stomach(s) tail tooth/teeth
brushing my
cutting
them
spreading
shake
thigh(s) thumbpad tits toe(s)
pinky
tongue(s)
golden-
mother
of flame
of the cultural imperialist
thick-
-tied
tip of my
your two
torso, half a tumor viscera voice(s) waist wings wrists

SIXTH: a data structure which enables sublinear-time lookup

never
ever

yesterday

earlier
a little less   too   **late**   at night
later on

for a   a little   **while**

and   Are you happy   around   by   Can you see her   come back   **now**
do it   here and   I hear it   I see it   just   now   **now**
of rain falling   right   Where are you   Where I live   **now**
now   -adays   -am-found   and now   like always   now   stoned
now   that I think of it   that you're thinking back   wewe   we're talking
you want to start

at any given   ever since the   for a   in another   not at the   **moment**
not since the   the maroon of the   this   **moment**
moment   at one, like this   one, at sunrise   her last, of vigor
moment   not one, too soon
of inspiration

every ten   in that split   ten   twenty-eight   **second**(s)   the one, I saw you

a   a couple of   about a   another   every   for a   **minute**(s)
forty-five   four   one skinny   three more   twenty   **minute**(s)
two   wait a   whole   **minute**(s)
minute   one, ago   one, before   one, later   without a little one lost

an   cocktail   eight or ten   every   every six   final   a half-   **hour**(s)
hour after   hour upon   next   telephone   thirteen   **hour**(s)
hour(s)   after hour   another one, after that   eight, a day   one, before
upon hour

2:05
so   **early**

before   cool   each cold   red-rivered   **dawn**

every   foggy   Monday   one   Sunday   this   tomorrow   **morning**
until   the wee ones, of the morning   Will There Really Be a   **morning**
morning   the one, after

before   **noon**

every   hypotenuse of   late   that   this   **afternoon**

midafternoon
four pm

an   all   coal gray   early   excruciatingly long   this   **evening**
evening   the, sky   time

half past eight

all   day and   day or   gypsy princess   last   late into the   **night**(s)
a nice quiet   on a cold   that superbly musicked   pretend   **night**
that   a thousand   Where were you last   tomorrow   **night**(s)

after   at   at around and ever after   by   **midnight**
midnight   on a, weary

birth-   carefree college   cold cloudy   the curtain of the   ever   **day**(s)
every   a gray July   hot flamenco   Joan of Arc   the many blue   old   **day**(s)
olden-   these   **day**(s)
day(s)   as one, is long   of due process   -time

early on   **Monday**
Friday
early on   **Tuesday**
Thursday
Saturday
Sunday
last   **Wednesday**

last   next   once a   this   **week**

weekend
fortnight

every frozen   a few   the following   the last two   the next   **month**(s)
over the course of   stealth weapon among   three   three more   **month**(s)
too many   **month**(s)
month(s)   of being frozen   one, later   six, old   sixteen, later   three, later
month(s)   untraceable, later

April   21
August
December
February
January
July
June
March
May   1
November
October
September

early   **fall**
disbelief in   a harbinger of   it's not yet   mistakes sink in   **spring**

spring break
mid- **summer**
winter

ever   every   for the first time in   for twenty-seven   four   **year**(s)
four hundred   freshman   Happy New   heavy-headed   over the   **year**(s)
the past   this   year afta   the yellow time of   **year**
year(s)   fifteen, ago   fifteen, later   in, year out   nine, of living
year(s)   ours, together   thirty, ago   thirty, later   to come   afta year
year   your first, of college

decade

thirteenth century
1597
seventeenth century
1990
1991
1992
1999

present   like the   the put-put of the   **past**   over, pending   the time

at   for   just   more than   never   **once**
once   a week   again   andf oral   and future   before
once   in a light-blue while   in a while   more   stony   -was-lost   upon a time

a hard   a Heidegger   a hell of a lot of   a hundred thousand million   **time**(s)
a long   a lot of   after all this   all   another   any   **time**
at the   at the same   at one and the same   besides   by the   each   **time**
earlier   eight more   elapsed   eleven   evening   every   **time**(s)
flashback to the   the first   for the first   for the last   for the rest of   **time**
free   having a good   if you have the   in   in former   it was   it's   **time**
its   many   next   nine   not losing any   once upon a   one last   **time**(s)
one-seventh of the   the only   other   out of   over   past the   **time**
real   the rest of   several   some   style of the   **time**(s)
that   this   to measure   the whole   **time**
time   a long, ago   after time   and time again   any, day or night
time   any, in the last two months   any, soon   goes by   have, to cook dinner
time   from, to   gone   immemorial   of year   off   one, and a place
time   to smile   time and, again

Want to come over   **tonight**   I can see   is the dress rehearsal
make like the sun   may it arrive   wake up   you'll tell her   **tomorrow**
tomorrow   I thought   is when   morning   now and, too   would not be too late

someday

fourth dimension
future

forever

SEVENTH: a descriptive piece of data associated with an image for retrieving that specific image from storage

Sun

 as tangerine on the horizon 12

 beginning to burn
  the fog off a curling infinitude 118

 in the hot 32

 lack of 16
 make like the 113
 Merc, its baby 136
 -rise 17
 scream whistles 66
 -set 17, 76, 88

 stingy, rounding the curve 24

 the warbled light of the 108

Symbolism 21, 145

Word(s) 12, 28, 48, 55, 74, 83, 84, 89, 94, 116, 127, 144

 all the ones the astronauts said 47
 and dissatisfaction 91
 bubble up, to affix to the fact 145

 finding 146
 for this? 97

 in other 72
 (the) last 174
 like *tears* 145

 the longest in the language 82
 the one not on the page

 playing with 146

 the same 73
 use of 93

 we never said a 26
 whose meaning might be unclear 20